The Illusion of Illusions

Sunita Pant Bansal is a renowned mythologist, storyteller and author with a career spanning over four decades. Throughout her journey, she has worn many hats, excelling as a writer, editor, publisher and entrepreneur.

She has headed publishing houses, and founded and edited newspapers and magazines for readers in India, the US and the UK. Her contributions to the world of literature extend across multiple platforms, working with prestigious organizations such as Walt Disney, Warner Bros., Pearson Education, *The Times of India*, *Hindustan Times*, and ABP Group.

In addition to her global collaborations, Sunita ran her own publishing house, creating books for audiences worldwide, and she served as the president of the esteemed Institute of Indology, further cementing her influence in the literary world.

Bestselling author of *Everyday Gita*, Sunita has authored over thirty-five books for adults and young readers, delving into the philosophy of mythology. She has also written innumerable children's books focused on folk literature and scriptures, which have been translated into multiple languages and sold across the globe. Her books explore and reinterpret timeless tales of characters from the epics and foundational texts for modern readers. Her storytelling blends mythology with history, making ancient tales accessible in today's context.

Sunita's contributions to publishing and literature have earned her widespread recognition, including the 2024 AALEKH Women Achievers Award.

Website: www.sunitapantbansal.com
LinkedIn & Instagram: @sunitapantbansal
X (earlier Twitter) & Facebook: @sunitapb

Also by Sunita Pant Bansal

KRISHNA The Management Guru

Everyday Gita

'When the stories of great men are told, the tales of the women in their lives often sink into obscurity. Sunita knits together a fascinating tale of Yashodara, the wife Prince Siddhartha left behind on his journey to becoming the Buddha, proving that there are different paths to the Buddha, and Yashodara's is one among them.'

Anand Neelakantan
bestselling author of the *Bahubali* trilogy

'While Prince Siddhartha's renunciation and enlightenment are the glory of Indian culture, lesser social mortals are conditioned to read his iconic journey as man's entitlement. Sunita Pant Bansal marvellously gives voice to Yashodara, releasing the concept of the Buddha from the prisons of patriarchal narrowness, making the philosophy wider and inclusive.'

Koral Dasgupta
author of *The Sati Series*

'The paths to nirvana are many. If the Buddha could achieve it through leaving his house in search of truth, his wife Yashodara achieved it through her commitment to the family as a single mother. Sunita brings out the unknown dimension of Yashodara in this path-breaking book. A must-read for everyone who wants to understand spirituality from the dimension of a committed wife and mother. You may find your path to nirvana in this book.'

Dr Radhakrishnan Pillai
bestselling author of *Corporate Chanakya,
Chanakya's 7 Secrets of Leadership,* and more

The Illusion of Illusions

The Story of Yashodara, Buddha's Wife

Sunita Pant Bansal

Published by
Rupa Publications India Pvt. Ltd 2025
7/16, Ansari Road, Daryaganj
New Delhi 110002

Sales centres:
Bengaluru Chennai
Hyderabad Jaipur Kathmandu
Kolkata Mumbai Prayagraj

Copyright © Sunita Pant Bansal 2025

All rights reserved.

This is a work of fiction. Names, characters, places and incidents are either the product of the author's imagination or are used fictitiously and any resemblance to any actual person, living or dead, events or locales is entirely coincidental.

No part of this publication may be reproduced, transmitted, or stored in a retrieval system, in any form or by any means, electronic, mechanical, photocopying, recording or otherwise, without the prior permission of the publisher.

P-ISBN: 978-93-6156-606-6
E-ISBN: 978-93-6156-509-0

First impression 2025

10 9 8 7 6 5 4 3 2 1

The moral right of the author has been asserted.

Printed in India

This book is sold subject to the condition that it shall not, by way of trade or otherwise, be lent, resold, hired out, or otherwise circulated, without the publisher's prior consent, in any form of binding or cover other than that in which it is published.

I would like to dedicate this story to married women all across the globe...

CONTENTS

Foreword / xi
Author's Note / xv
Prologue / xix
1. The Son-rise / 1
2. The Beginning / 18
3. Growing Up / 28
4. Togetherness / 50
5. Abandonment / 74
6. Acceptance / 93
7. Homecoming / 112
8. Departure / 124
9. Farewell / 148
10. The Sangha / 165
11. Alone Again / 178
12. Last Meeting / 193

Acknowledgements / 213

FOREWORD

'*Buddham saranam gacchami…*' the echo of that sonorous chant has wafted through the air of many centuries, and Gautama Buddha, the prince-turned-visionary mendicant, is among the most venerated persons in human civilization. Not many have asked about the home he left behind, a young wife Yashodara, and their newborn son, Rahul. Sunita Pant Bansal enters this precinct with her daring novel *The Illusion of Illusions: Yashodara's Story,* charting the path of the woman who suddenly found herself bereft of traditional support, and unprepared to surrender her beloved to the pedestal of public worship. Famous personages have no secrets; hence, a plethora of literature on the Buddha and Buddhism's various strands is easily traceable. On the other hand, women who are 'married to greatness' face challenges of self-definition and social navigation that have seldom evoked curiosity. Lately, creative writers are exploring such interstices, and highly engrossing books on women in mythology, legend and folklore are emerging with regularity. On Yashodara, Sunita Pant Bansal's is among the first novels to appear in Indian writing in English, alongside Hindi writer Maithili Sharan Gupt (1886–1964) who wrote a touching poem about Yashodara's surrender of her son Rahul to monkhood.

Sunita Bansal redefines Yashodara's journey. Suddenly separated from her childhood companion Siddharth whom she later marries, the abandoned wife can turn into a dependent member of a larger family or can strike out on her own path. Without violating the barebones of the narrative we have inherited from storytellers, Sunita tracks Yashodara's evolution from a puzzled and bereft wife to a spiritual leader in her own right. With unhesitating candour, Sunita says in the author's note, 'The story starts with the enlightened Buddha meeting an enlightened Yashodara, and ends with Yashodara attaining nirvana before the Buddha.' Such a trajectory is based on the clouded history of the Buddhist nuns—originators of the oral forms that later became known as the *Therigatha* (verses of the elder nuns)— the earliest examples of women addressing spirituality, with some enunciations going back to the sixth century BCE. Anonymous, undated, amorphous but powerful, one may reasonably assume that Buddhism had a place for women devotees. Sunita Pant Bansal uses this leverage of the possible to construct a story of how the Buddha's foster mother, Queen Pajapati, and wife Yashodara established independent *sangha*s or monasteries for women. One reason was that Buddhism initially discouraged women from joining the order, and the novel describes large gatherings waiting at the gates of spiritual centres, hoping to be allowed admission. Denied such favour, the women started chiselling their own path under the guidance of women leaders. Yashodara discovered and propagated the idea of compassion, and reached out to the suffering multitudes with herbal medicines and soothing words. Queen Pajapati offered shelter to women shunned by society. Without sounding essentialist, the novel emphasizes the nurturing role of women, and the intellectual pursuits of men in the monastic orders.

The novelist's inventiveness shows up most impressively in the delicate and tender moments when the Buddha meets his wife Yashodara. During his first visit to the palace after being absent for seven years, they converse privately, Yashodara holding firmly to her dignity and not allowing any words of recrimination to slip out. Another time, in answer to her son's questions about his father, Yashodara urges him to ask the Buddha for his 'inheritance'. Consequently, Rahul adopts monkhood, and Yashodara loses another vital relationship. These experiences make her intellectually and emotionally stronger, and in connecting with other women in the household, and the community, she gains a wider understanding of the human predicament than she would have within the confines of royal privilege. The parallel with the Buddha's process of gaining emancipatory knowledge through seeing illness, suffering and death, is Yashodara's exchanges with women on the oppressions, dishonour and discriminations thrust upon them. Kisa and Amrapali are sufficient examples. Knowledge leads to introspection, self-purification and finally Enlightenment, if one is fortunate. The architect of her own destiny, Yashodara emerges 'victorious' from the crucible of her distress to adopt the humble role of a leader to a community of women, discovering a common sisterhood in abandonment by society in one form or another. When she meets the Buddha finally, the beloved who was Prince Siddharth to her at one time, this is what the novelist imagines:

> 'I am my own refuge,' I said to him. 'It has been more than four decades when you told me about the three refuges you taught people...*buddha, dhamma* and *sangha*. Going beyond all those, I have discovered my own refuge in my own self. I have come to thank you for showing the way.'

Sunita Pant Bansal's novel, *The Illusion of Illusions: Yashodara's Story*, is an engrossing read, a thoughtful intervention into an apocryphal tale, and a therapeutic ode to women's unrecorded triumphs. It is a welcome addition to the growing corpus of lost legends about women earlier written out of history.

Professor Malashri Lal
Member, General Council, and Convener, English Advisory Board, Sahitya Akademi, Govt of India
Former Head, Department of English and Director, Women's Studies and Development Centre,
University of Delhi,
New Delhi
13 November 2023

AUTHOR'S NOTE

I have been obsessed with the Buddha's story since I was twelve years old, since I read about his leaving his sleeping wife and son. I was actually angry with him for abandoning his family. Hence, over the years I read whatever I could lay my hands on, related to the Buddha, his life, his travels, his sermons, the jatakas, everything, till I understood why he did whatever he did.

Sometime in the late 1900s, I started getting dreams and visions that seemed to be related to the Buddha's life, which made me go on a Buddhist pilgrimage to explore all the sites associated with him physically. I documented that journey in a book called *On the Footsteps of Buddha*, but I was not satisfied. Something was still missing. I decided to write another book—this time recording the Buddha's emotional journey. This was in 2006.

While writing, I realized that Yashodara was peeping from behind the haze of words—all the time—till I could not ignore her. I was so distracted that I left the story midway and subsequently forgot about it.

During the Covid lockdown of 2020, I was going through my archives and discovered the abandoned story of the Buddha's inner journey. I went through my notes again. This time, there was no confusion. The fourteen years

xvi « *The Illusion of Illusions*

that had elapsed had pushed me through the wringer of life in a way that taught me many valuable lessons.

It was clear to me that it was Yashodara who wanted her story told, and I was ready to tell it. All my research, my travel notes, my visions and dreams actually pointed towards her! Like a giant jigsaw puzzle, everything fell into place, and I started writing *The Illusion of Illusions: Yashodara's Story*.

The narrative begins with Siddharth the Buddha arriving home after his enlightenment. Following this, a meeting with his wife Yashodara triggers a flashback, where we travel to Siddharth and Yashodara's birth and their childhood years, and their interactions during that time.

The story continues, interspersed with flashbacks exploring Yashodara and Siddharth's past, their time spent together, and the various red flags that she misses during the thirteen years of their marriage. Through her eyes, we witness her husband's transformation from a sheltered, reticent prince into a man with a mission. We also witness her joys and sorrows, her expectations and frustrations, her fairytale wedding, and her overwhelming devastation at the departure of her husband on the day of the birth of their son, pushing her into a cavernous pit of depression.

Yashodara's character is powerful and multi-layered. When Siddharth leaves his family and home to explore and understand the illusory world, he leaves behind a disillusioned Yashodara. So, while her husband consciously pursues enlightenment outside the palace, Yashodara unconsciously pursues the same within her home and family. Hers is the tougher path. And yet, she also becomes the Buddha when her husband does, putting a question mark on the very course the Buddha had chosen to attain his Buddhahood.

The story starts with the enlightened Buddha meeting an enlightened Yashodara, and ends with Yashodara attaining nirvana before the Buddha.

Writing the story in Yashodara's voice was a challenge, no doubt, but it was also a phenomenally cathartic experience, one that I will cherish all my life. Mapping the fictional story onto historical facts was yet another challenge, but an exhilarating educational experience in itself.

Yashodara's voice, her story, is one that every woman can and will relate to. I hope this humble effort of mine will help many break through their illusions and be free to live as their own selves, in their own bodies, and on their own terms.

PROLOGUE

Tonight, I am going to die.

No, do not be surprised. For some decades now, I have known about my earlier lives and my relationship with Siddharth in those. This life, for both of us, is our last on this plane. I am also aware that I will leave when my work here is done.

It has been over forty years now since I have been chronicling my life for posterity. Tonight, the last words will be added and I will be free to leave.

This morning, I went to pay my final obeisance to Siddharth the Buddha, and thanked him for leading me to myself. It was an eventful journey and worth every breath of mine.

'I am my own refuge,' I said to him. 'It has been more than four decades since you told me about the three refuges you taught people…*buddha*, *dhamma* and *sangha*. Going beyond all those, I have discovered my own refuge in my own self. I have come to thank you for showing the way.'

He was surprised neither by my visit nor by my declaration. He never is…because he always knows.

'We both came to this earth for a reason. You have completed your task; I still have some more left to do.

You are the truth, Yasho, you are the way. And you are free to leave, you know that too.'

I returned to my room to finish this journal—the story of my life, my experiences and reflections that I started writing the day my son decided to follow his father. That was the day the fog started clearing from my own path too.

I do not give discourses. I have dialogues with those who want to talk to me or have unanswered questions. I like to engage with people. When I step out, it is to see the world, the marvels of nature, and the living beings, which include people too. I return to sit here and record my observations.

One day, I hope these words of mine will help someone somewhere find their refuge from this delusional world of illusions.

Meanwhile, let me take you to the point of time and place where I started reflecting on my life exclusively. Because before that my son was the focus of my life, or so I believed.

1

THE SON-RISE

I was as ready as I ever could be, as I ever was—since the day I was born perhaps, thirty-six long years ago. Today, sitting on the cold marble bench in my balcony at 4 a.m., I felt a soft breeze, soft as the breath of a mother.

Normally that time of the morning is very still; the air also stops flowing, and the gentle warmth of mother earth can be felt. It's very comforting. Today, with the warmth was an added breath of air, more like a sigh of a mother having just delivered her baby. The trees, too, seemed to droop and sigh in unison, as though they had also just dropped their ripe fruits on the ground.

Having nurtured the baby in her womb for nine months, the mother lets go of it, severing the umbilical cord, handing over the newborn to the world—as I did seven years ago. Today, again, I was going through the same labour pains as I did that fateful evening when my son was born at sunset.

And the sun set in our lives.

That sun was going to rise today, lighting up the Shakya

capital of Kapilvastu. But my sun will set yet again, this time forever.

My rooms in the palace face the east. I wake up every morning at 3 a.m. and prepare for my morning contemplation and prayers. My prayers are more like talking to Mother Goddess, expressing my gratitude rather than asking for or complaining about anything.

'This is the time when nature also goes still in meditation, the gates of heaven open up, and gods are waiting to welcome us. This is when communion with gods happens.' My mother had said that when I asked her once why she woke up so early to pray, and I firmly believed her.

'That is why it is also considered an auspicious time to enter the world or leave it,' she had added.

After the morning ruminations, I love to sit in my balcony to watch the sunrise. All along the railing, my favourite, the enchanting pink and white creeping roses lift up their fragrant little heads to give me company.

That is also the time when the moisture released from the air settles as drops of dew on the flower petals and leaves. Many times I have heard, or maybe imagined hearing, the melodious sound of the falling dewdrops.

The last seven years have taught me one very valuable thing—never to shut my eyes. Even when I sleep with my eyes shut, it's only my physical body that sleeps; I am awake. I am always aware of every little movement outside my room as well as inside it, enveloped in the comforting sounds of silence and the pitch darkness of the night.

Last night was different. My body did not sleep. I lay with my eyes wide open, waiting for the day to dawn, with mixed feelings of excitement and sadness. I was excited because I was going to meet my heartbeat, and sad because I knew I would lose a piece of my heart again today.

Deep down, my heart still encased a secret yearning for my husband. My love for him was immeasurable like the sky; seven years were but seven moments in that timelessness. Even now, I could trace his handsomely chiselled face with my fingers…in my imagination. A face with a slightly crooked nose, his long earlobes that were better suited to earrings than my small ones, as I always told him, and his full lips, which when they broke into a smile never failed to make my heart flutter.

Pushing aside the distracting thoughts, I sat up and decided to freshen up and get ready for my morning reflections.

Donning my favourite white hand-woven muslin robes, I sat on the floor on a jute mat to watch my breath, the life force that connects us all, that also connects Siddharth and me. With each breath I inhaled and exhaled, I could feel the throbbing of life within every cell of my body. Yet, amidst all that connection I felt disconnected.

Steeped in my perceptions of the never-ending marvels of nature, I heard the koels start their morning chorus. As I went out to sit in my balcony, the bulbuls joined the koels, and more and more birds started chirping, as if on cue, asking the sun to wake up.

The sun was waking up, though slowly, ray by ray. It began with a pinkish glow, almost like a gradually spreading blush, as though it had done something naughty the night before and was too shy to come out.

Everything seemed different today, the sun too. It was behaving like a coy bride coming out of her room to face the world with her new, now woman's eyes, brimming with love. The love that was spilling over and spreading, and spreading, and touching everything, every soul coming its way, colouring them in its own colour, enveloping the cosmos in its loving embrace.

And then… The lover and the loved became one—and everything came alive—shining in the shared glow of the love of bride and groom, the glow of fulfilment.

I could hear the buzz of servants preparing for the big event. In fact, the entire city, the entire populace was busy cleaning up their homes and themselves, including the birds and beasts, to celebrate the homecoming of their favourite son.

The sun was now ready to face the world. As I sat watching this, mesmerized, suddenly everything went unusually quiet—the leaves stopped rustling, the birds, animals, people, all were silent with bated breath. I went up to the balcony's railing.

And then I saw it.

Far in the horizon, a speck of ochre rose up, growing like the sun. This was the sunrise I was waiting for today—the rise of the son of Kapilvastu.

A bird flew towards it and then turned back chattering excitedly, as though informing her clan. A wave of happiness could be seen, and felt, in nature. The flowers began to bloom, spreading their fragrance, the birds sang in unison like a choir; even the trees swayed rhythmically.

Somebody standing at the highest point of the palace

shouted, 'Here he comes!' Surprisingly, no one else shouted, and everyone became deferential, expectation writ large on their faces.

The ochre spot had turned into a wave by now, an ochre wave of flowing robes of a thousand monks.

The wave entered the city...led by the Buddha.

Along with it entered a ray of bright sunlight through the balcony into my room, like a blessing, or maybe a message, telling me something, showing a path.

Just like today, twenty years ago, somebody standing at the highest point of the palace must have seen the grand wedding procession approaching too. The procession that had brought me here to this palace, which became more my home than the one I was born in.

How apprehensive, yet happy, I was. It was a dream come true for me. I was sixteen years old, as was Siddharth, my husband, the prince of Kapilvastu. I had married the most sought-after bachelor in the kingdom. I was the envy of every girl and the pride of my family. All this made me happy, but I was apprehensive of entering a new family, a new household, of handling my new responsibilities. After all, I was a princess now. Surely there must be a different set of rules for royalty, I thought.

Siddharth and I had practically grown up together, as our families were good friends. My mother Pamita was a distant cousin of King Shuddhodhan, so we were treated like extended family. I visited the palace a lot as a child but never dreamt of living in it permanently, ever.

Once I became a teenager and got my period, my visits to the palace stopped. My mother started grooming me, as per the socio-cultural obligation of our times. I still recall the time when she forcibly braided my hair and made me wear a long, embroidered dress. We had to attend a function in the palace and I felt very uncomfortable, more so when I found the young boys staring at me. They were the same boys with whom I had climbed trees and played games! That was the first time I realized that girls were different from boys.

I hated growing up. My father, Suppabuddha, was not like the other traditional fathers. He indulged me, taught me to swim, ride a horse, use a bow and arrow, and even defend myself with a sword. Above else, my father taught me to question everything boldly and critically; he encouraged my curiosity.

'Don't swallow the words of your teachers blindly as words of wisdom. Those words remain hollow if your mind doesn't engage with them. So, question them till you understand them fully,' he would say.

Though this nature of mine was deemed stubbornness or rebelliousness by some, retrospectively speaking, it was this very questioning-everything attitude that saw me through the turbulent times of my life.

Though my mother taught me how to cook, clean, sew, embroider, knit, and even prepare body scrubs from pulses and seeds, she also taught me that girls were as powerful or strong as boys.

'A woman's power is not about handling weapons; it's not in our muscles. Our power may not be seen or measured, but it's fierce. We have a blazing fire in our wombs. That is the source of our power, our strength.' My mother's words echoed in my heart whenever I felt weak. Today was one such moment.

I had realized long ago what she meant. The fact that a woman creates or can create a life within her is an empowering thought. Mother reinforced it further by pointing out that we always addressed earth as Mother Earth for a reason. We depend on her for our sustenance, our very existence. Hence, all our festivals and rituals are centred on her. This observation gave me a lot of strength.

'Women are goddesses then!' was my happy conclusion as a young girl.

'Maybe, maybe not!' was my mother's cryptic response.

I gathered myself and went back into the room. The lone ray of sunlight had by now turned into a stream of light, reaching up to my bed.

And so did Rahul, my seven-year-old son, the current prince of Kapilvastu, the designated heir of his grandfather King Shuddhodhan.

'How are you, darling?' I asked, gesturing him to sit beside me on the bed.

He did not answer. Today, this otherwise babbling boy was silent. He sat with his head bowed, the tiny soft fingers of his small right hand tracing over the embroidery of my bedspread. While contemplating the immense, seemingly insurmountable issues that his seven-year-old brain faced sometimes, Rahul had a tendency to either curl a lock of his hair around his finger or trace the indentations of any surface at hand.

I gently caressed his silky black hair that he had inherited from me. He looked up. His large dark eyes were spilling over with unsaid emotions. For a split second he reminded me of the young, newly married Siddharth with his never-ending questions.

'Who is he, mother? The one everyone is scared to talk about?'

'Are you scared too, my son?'

'No, I am not scared. I am wondering… I had a glimpse of him from my window, as he entered the palace grounds. He was shining so bright, as though covered with gold. While everybody walked, he seemed to be gliding, barely touching the ground. How can anyone be scared of such a person! That's what I have been wondering. But then, everyone at the palace does seem to be scared of something. What could it be, mother? And who is he? Who is he to us?'

There was an innocent perplexity in Rahul's voice. He had never seen his father, but now the genetic pull was surfacing. Blood is thicker than water, they say; it was certainly being proved today, right at this very moment.

I hugged my son instinctively, knowing where this whirlpool was taking us. He hugged me back with equal fervour, somehow sharing my secret knowledge, unknowingly.

'The monk you saw is your father, son.'

'Prince Siddharth? My Baba?' Rahul looked excited now, though a tad confused.

He must have visualized his father as the prince that he was, and dressed appropriately, somewhat like his grandfather—or Dada, as he called him—King Shuddhodhan.

'Yes…he had to go on a very special mission, seven years ago…'

'Oh, I remember that!' he cut me short. 'Dada has told me many stories of his time before he left. He says I am a lot like Baba, but then also not like him in some ways. Is Baba back now? Will he live with us? He doesn't look like a prince though. What should I say to him?'

Even as Rahul rattled off these questions in his inimitable manner, he looked happy yet doubtful.

'I don't think so, son. Your Baba doesn't belong to us alone any more. He belongs to the whole world. He is not Prince Siddharth any more, he is the Buddha now.'

This was the gut-wrenching truth spilling from my mouth, though how I wished it wasn't! I just wanted to go back in time and wipe out the last seven years of my life. Somehow the yearning of my heart kept peeking out now and then, like a sapling looking for sunlight.

Rewinding my life back by seven years reminded me how Siddharth had the power to change me easily and instantly, with just a couple of words or a smile. It made me happy then, but today it terrified me…to lose control over myself like that. No, I must not become soft now, I admonished myself. I owed it to my son, as well as my husband, to be the reflection of their strength.

Coming back to Rahul…what should a son say to his father who left him the moment he was born?

'Go and meet him, Rahul. Tell him who you are, and ask for your inheritance.'

I don't know why I said this. Maybe because this was the only way the cloud of confusion that was hovering over us for the past one year would finally part to reveal the right path.

Last year, at about the same time, we received information that my husband Siddharth had attained enlightenment, and was being called the Buddha. It was good news, for that was why he had left us, hadn't he? And he was successful in finding what he was looking for. In fact, it was a significant piece of news for humanity at large.

Unfortunately, Siddharth's father did not take kindly to this information. King Shuddhodhan was a father first before anything else. Had his son failed in his mission, there could have been some hope of him returning home, however slim. With him becoming the Buddha, all hopes of his ever coming home were shattered forever. The king of Kapilvastu had lost his son.

Since that moment, King Shuddhodhan's focus shifted to his grandson, Rahul. What he couldn't make out of Siddharth, he wanted to make of his son.

'What Siddharth did, renouncing his birthright, our family name, is unpardonable. I don't want his son to be like him. That would not be the right example of a role model to follow. I have decided to start Rahul's training soon. This time, it will be serious training under the right master in a hermitage. My grandson must train as a warrior, in order to become my successor,' the king had declared.

A six-year-old was too young to be sent away to train as a warrior! My mother-in-law Queen Pajapati managed to convince her husband to give their grandson another year at the palace. And I'm fairly certain that this permission must have been granted most reluctantly by the king.

I do not know what kind of personal relationship the king and the queen shared; it was certainly not like that of my parents. I would see more deference than affection in Pajapati for her husband, unlike my parents, who showed their affection for each other quite unabashedly. I shrugged it off, assuming that it was the way of the royals.

Queen Pajapati's sole purpose in life seemed to be pampering her husband and son with food. She had no interest in the affairs of the court or the kingdom. She saw to it that her son was busy being happy, and happy being busy. Little did she know that her darling son was too clever to let her know or see anything other than what she wanted to see.

Once we were married, Siddharth found the soulmate he was looking for, as did I, to share his heart and soul with. That's why, even now, after seven years, I still feel a twinge in my heart recalling his leaving me without as much as whispering goodbye.

Anyway, coming back to Pajapati…she wasted no time in taking up the reins of our lives, and in the last seven years, she was a pillar of strength not only for me and my son, but also for the king. She became her husband's backbone. It was an amazing transformation for a person who had no interest in the court or the ruling of the kingdom, to now be seen with her husband at all times.

As far as the king was concerned, he was blinded by his own grief and anger. He had never really acknowledged how his pride was wounded by Siddharth's leaving. As a father, he could never let go of his expectations. This bitterness was very damaging. It made him want to control his grandson, not realizing that control, more often than not, led to outcomes contrary to the ones desired.

Initially I felt the same as my father-in-law. I was deeply hurting and was full of anger against the injustice meted out to me by my fate, or so I thought. It was a very selfish notion.

But gradually, as I saw my son grow up, fatherless, I felt it was necessary for him to meet his father at least once, if only to know that he was not a fatherless child.

Today, though I was still unsure about my own meeting with my husband, I was quite sure about my son's need to meet his father.

Janaki, Rahul's maid, came to fetch him to get him ready for the grand meeting. It warmed my heart to see my son chattering excitedly about dressing up to meet his father. For me, it was the high point of the past seven years; a glorious moment celebrating my success as a mother.

It was once he turned two and started playing with the children of other families living in the palace that Rahul realized the absence of his father. He saw the other children go back home to their mothers and fathers, whereas he only had his mother to return to.

This was when I realized that I couldn't remain angry and hurt forever. I had a responsibility towards my son. My father always said that children do not ask to be born; it's we who bring them into this world. Therefore, it is our duty to look after them till they are able to look after themselves. He often showed me how even animals tended to their young till they became strong enough to go out into the world.

I remember how we once looked after a pigeon's nest inside an old box, saving it from cats and rabbits, till the mother pigeon saw to it that her squabs were fit to fly. Even a cat looks after her kittens for a couple of months, till they are old enough to fend for themselves. Why, even a tree holds on to its fruit till it is ripe enough to let go!

I was no different from the other living creatures of nature. Like them, I had a natural duty towards my baby, and I intended to carry it out to the best of my ability. I had to look after him till he was capable of doing so himself. Little did I know then how short a period that would be.

I started telling my son stories about his father. I told him how the pain and suffering of other living beings hurt him, and how it bothered him so much that he decided to go and find a cure for it.

Knowing that his father existed made a huge difference in Rahul's life. He could now say that his father was travelling for work. He regained whatever self-confidence he might have lost during the first few weeks or months that he played with other children in the palace.

As was the custom in royal families, Rahul's foundational education started once he turned four. Tutors came to the palace to teach him through stories, either by enacting them or by using puppets. Storytelling was the preferred mode of teaching till the child was six, after which a more formal approach was employed that involved testing the child periodically.

I was proud to note that my son excelled in everything, and he took an exceptional interest in the crafts. In fact, we spent a lot of time together creating all kinds of objects with wood as well as clay.

Those were fun days indeed...how fast children grow!

Rahul matured faster than his age and became very protective of me. It was a pleasant feeling, though it made me miss my husband more.

Siddharth was losing out on experiencing fatherhood, I thought sadly. But then, he would be a father to a larger flock in the times to come, I explained to myself. So, actually it was Rahul's loss, not his father's, and I was not willing to allow that.

As humans we are brought up believing that we need both parents for the healthy, well-rounded growth of a child. Who made those rules? Nature certainly did not. The males of all species of animals and birds seem to be responsible only for providing food for their family. If observed carefully, the skills for survival are learnt by the animal itself. In fact, they are not even learnt, they are buried within the animal and discovered by it when faced with a crisis. The mothers nurture their young ones, and in that process, instil self-confidence in them to discover their own survival instincts.

Over the years, humans somehow divided their life skills into soft indoor ones, to be taught by mothers to their children, and hard outdoor ones, to be taught by the fathers. Maybe this division of labour happened when humans started getting formally married.

Coming back to the moot point, I decided that as father, Siddharth would provide food—in our case, spiritual nourishment. And I would nurture my son, enabling him to discover his own capabilities.

Rohini, my maid, my shadow of twenty years, pulled me out of my reverie by gently touching my shoulder.

'Tell me all!' I commanded, before she could say anything.

Rohini, usually the epitome of calmness, looked quite disoriented. I had to direct the conversation to make any sense out of it.

'Your Highness, it's your husband, Prince Siddharth! He has changed completely. They call him the Awakened One…' Rohini started off by stating the obvious, to my impatience.

'Since last night, preparations have been going on in the kitchen to prepare a grand feast for the prince and his followers. I couldn't sleep the whole night, as the aromas were so delicious!'

'How many people have come with him?' I interjected, before Rohini could digress further into a long-winded description of the menu.

'Oh, Your Highness, there must be more than a thousand people in all. In fact, all the men missing from the palace are with the prince now. I'm sorry—I shouldn't call him the prince any more; he is the Buddha."

'Are you saying that Anand and Anirudh have also come?'

'Yes, Your Highness, and so have the other men, husbands and brothers of people working in the palace. You wouldn't know, but in the last few months, most of the young men from the palace left to join the Buddha. All of them have become shaven-headed monks like him.'

Saying that I was shocked to get this news would be an understatement. I had absolutely no idea that Siddharth's fame was so widespread. More than fame, it seemed like his allure was pulling people away from their families. More than a thousand and still growing...how many more Siddharths would the Buddha spawn! My heart started beating erratically, and I put my palms on the bed to support myself. No, this was no time to feel weak.

'A lavish feast was laid out in the grand hall for the Buddha and his followers. Since their numbers were more than double the estimate, the feast was extended out into the royal lawns. His Highness invited his son to join him at the head of the royal table for the celebratory feast, but the Buddha declined, as did his followers. He said, "We have eaten today." You see, the monks eat only once a day!' Rohini's eyes seemed to have widened forever.

Continuing to look dazed, Rohini rambled on, 'Then His Highness saw a begging bowl in the Buddha's hands, and commented, "We Shakyas do not beg." The Buddha promptly responded, "I am now one of those who beg." Oh my God, I have never seen His Highness looking so sorrowful as he did then!'

It may seem a very odd reaction to some, but I felt awash with a wave of relief. My father-in-law must have finally understood that his son was not his anymore. This closure was very important for him.

Begging was a spiritual practice that helped a monk liberate himself from the consciousness of the self, which meant that neither did he have pride, nor did he indulge in self-deprecation. Such a practice demolished all caste or class differences among people.

The son had wiped out his father's arrogance with one single stroke of his own humility.

'Your Highness, they have asked you to join them in the grand hall,' Rohini finally delivered the message she was sent to deliver.

'No Rohini, I will not leave this room. If my husband wants to meet me, he will come here to do so, I am sure.'

I had no intention of facing my husband after seven years in a hall full of people.

There was no rush. I had waited for so long, a few more minutes or hours wouldn't hurt. As Rohini left, I went back to sit in the balcony, in the familiar warm comfort of the sun's rays and the *kutrook-kutrook-kutrook* of the green-brown barbets.

It was a bright, sunny morning that day.

2

THE BEGINNING

I was born in Kapilvastu to Pamita, wife of Suppabuddha, a wealthy landlord. My mother was a distant cousin of King Shuddhodhan of Kapilvastu, and our family was, therefore, treated as the extended family of the king. My father was also of a royal lineage, but he had chosen a different path.

Kapilvastu was the capital of the Shakya kingdom at the foothills of the Himalayas, with rich and powerful neighbours like the kingdoms of Kosal and Magadh. The important cities of Kosal were its capital Sravasti, former capital Ayodhya, and the pilgrimage city of Benares. Magadh was known for its wealth of iron ore, which was procured not far from its capital of Rajgriha.

Kapilvastu's landscape was thickly wooded in the north towards the mountains, gradually flattening out southwards into paddy fields dotted with villages and towns.

Siddharth was born the same day I was, but in Lumbini. His mother Queen Maya was travelling to her parents' house, when she stopped on the way in the Sal forest of Lumbini to rest. There she gave birth to Siddharth.

Unfortunately, she didn't keep well after her return to Kapilvastu and passed away seven days later.

Queen Maya's younger sister, Pajapati, took over the responsibility of looking after the week-old baby. Though King Shuddhodhan married Pajapati, he could not get over the loss of his beloved wife Maya. He declared a mourning period of forty days in the kingdom. So, neither Siddharth's birth nor the king's second marriage was celebrated.

My father was very upset by all this, but mainly because he couldn't celebrate my birth with the grand feast that he had planned since the day I was conceived. It was the peak summer of Vaishakh, and the intense heat didn't do much to help my father's frustration.

Anyway, though the celebrations did not happen, the rituals had to be followed. We were taken to the temple on the eleventh day of our birth, to be named by the priest. After praying to the Mother Goddess, the priest studied our horoscopes and gave us names fitting our natal charts. The little prince was named Siddharth, meaning 'one who attains it all'. I was named Yashodara, meaning 'one who is full of splendour'.

And it rained that day, the first rain of monsoons. Since rain on any auspicious occasion is considered God's blessings, the moods cooled down—my father's as well as King Shuddhodhan's—changing for the better.

My father told me that the king had blessed me along with his son, saying, 'May you comfort each other forever.' I think our bond was established then. Or, maybe we were born on the same day because we already had a bond from our past lives…

Here, I must mention that there was something about the astrological predictions for Siddharth that I had no clue about, until after I got married. But before that, we must hear Queen Maya's story.

Queen Maya, Siddharth's mother, was King Shuddhodhan's first wife, and the love of his life. Maya's father was King Anjana of the neighbouring Koliya kingdom that lay to the southeast of the Shakya kingdom, beyond the river Rohini. Incidentally, Anjana was also a distant cousin of Shuddhodhan. In those times, everybody in the royal families across kingdoms was related to each other. Siddharth and I were also related—technically speaking, that is.

Let us go back to the very beginning, to the day Siddharth was supposedly conceived.

It was the twentieth spring of Maya and Shuddhodhan's marriage.

One day, as Maya lay on her soft bed, head resting on semul pillows, partially covered with fine silk sheets, she started hearing soft music, which sounded like gently flowing water. There was a flowery fragrance in the air, as though thousands of flowers had suddenly bloomed together. Maya felt a deep intoxication within her. Wanting to be alone, she sent away her maids.

After a while, Maya saw a six-headed white elephant descending from the sky. The elephant was white as the pristine snow of the mountain peaks, surprisingly ethereal, and was carrying a pink lotus in one of its trunks. It approached Maya, and she was enveloped by that apparition. Then, she felt an ever so light touch on her right side, like a gentle nudge or a slight brush against her waist. A shiver of excitement ran through Maya's entire being. Then the elephant disappeared, or rather dematerialized.

The whole thing happened so fast that it seemed like a dream to Maya. But she was left with an unexplainable ecstasy. Was it a vision, a visitation, or merely a dream? It did not really matter to her.

The next morning, Queen Maya woke up with a feeling of happiness that she had never felt before. She narrated her experience of the night to her husband. King Shuddhodhan called it a dream, but nevertheless wanted to understand its meaning.

He conferred with his coterie of intellectuals. I must add here that dreams were an important part of our lives and were considered to be cosmic messages.

'Congratulations! The queen is pregnant. You will have a son who is destined to rule the four corners of the world,' they assured the king. But then, they added a rider: 'If your son lives the life of a householder, he will become king of the material world. But if he leaves the house, he will become king of the incorporeal world.'

Why should his son leave the palace! The king found the idea itself to be absurd and brushed it aside. He and his wife had been waiting for an heir to the throne for twenty long years. The gods had apparently heard them, finally.

Months passed by blissfully. Once the baby was due, Queen Maya left for her parents' place in the Koliyan capital Devadaha for the delivery, as was the custom of those times.

On the way, near the Sal forest of Lumbini, Maya was seized by an immense desire to stop. She alighted from her palanquin. The forest was full of reddish-pink blooms, flowering in unnatural profusion.

Maya walked up to a pond to freshen herself. While bathing, she was gripped by the pangs of childbirth. She got out of the pond and walked up to a tree. Her maids and companions surrounded her as she gave birth, while standing, to a bonny baby boy.

The full moon was shining in all its glory, and the gods seemed to be blessing the birth. The birds were singing, the flowers were blooming, there was fragrance in the air and the musical sound of water—the entirety of nature seemed to be celebrating. Maya was very happy, but she sensed that she was not going to live for long. On returning to Kapilvastu, she requested her younger sister Pajapati to look after the baby as her own.

Maya passed away seven days after her son's birth. King Shuddhodhan was devastated, though he took Pajapati as his second wife and stepmother to his son, to honour his dead wife's wishes.

I was born on the same day as Siddharth, but without any drama.

My mother gave birth to me at home, under the supervision of a midwife and her helper. There was no fuss. The family astrologer promptly cast my horoscope and assured my parents that I had a very bright future ahead. He also predicted that I would be free from sickness, would marry into a rich family, and bear a son. What more could any parent ask for! It was a pity though that they could not celebrate this, because of the mourning declared by the king.

Now, coming back to Siddharth.

Unable to handle the loss of his wife, and unmindful of the birth of his son, a very disturbed King Shuddhodhan conferred with his astrologers again. He wanted to know if his son was as inauspicious as he thought him to be. It was very typical to blame the baby for the death of his mother, and the king was no different.

The royal astrologers congregated. They checked and rechecked Siddharth's birth chart but the verdict was the same. The boy was a born leader. In fact, his stars were very favourable for the kingdom. There was nothing inauspicious in the child's horoscope.

There was a young astrologer, though, who had some doubts. According to him, the child would face a dilemma of choosing one of the two options available to him. He could either go out and become a spiritual leader, or stay in and become the temporal leader. The other astrologers brushed aside this theory as they didn't see any reason why the royal prince, and heir to the throne of Kapilvastu, should go out in the first place.

The young astrologer, Kondanna, was barely in his teens, which could also be a reason why his so-called experienced seniors did not take him too seriously. Kondanna later became one of Siddharth's ardent followers.

While the debate among the astrologers was taking place, Sage Asit came to bless the baby and congratulate King Shuddhodhan. Asit was the most venerable sage in the kingdom, and the king was filled with gratitude at his visit. The sage had not only been the king's teacher but was also his father King Sihahanu's advisor and chaplain.

So, Shuddhodhan was certain that the revered sage would put all his doubts to rest.

To everyone's surprise, when Sage Asit saw the baby, he broke into tears and bowed his head to touch the baby's tiny feet, instead of touching the baby's head in the conventional style of blessing. The king was shocked to see the sage behaving like this. He felt his worst fears could be true and asked if the sage foresaw any misfortune coming their way through his son. After all, the baby's mother did die a week after his birth, which could not be considered auspicious under any circumstances.

'Is my son born to bring me sorrow?'

'Oh no! I am crying for myself. He will grow up to eliminate the darkness of ignorance from this world and I will not be able to witness that, as my life is drawing to a close,' the sage responded emotionally. 'Your son will rule the world with the light of his knowledge.'

King Shuddhodhan was relieved to hear Sage Asit's words, because he heard what he wanted to hear. 'Rule the world' was the key phrase here.

It came to be known later that soon after leaving the palace, Sage Asit set about preparing his nephew Nalaka to receive Siddharth's teachings in the future—that's how sure he was about his own predictions.

Siddharth would have grown up in a normal environment, if one of the royal astrologers had not reminded the king of the previous predictions and advised that the prince be kept away from pain or sorrow. His simple logic was, why take chances at all if things could be avoided!

This resulted in the palace being turned into a dreamland

for the prince to grow up in. The gardeners worked around the clock to remove any old, decayed or dead plant, leaf or flower. No old or sick person from the royal staff was allowed to enter the palace or its grounds: they had to leave the palace premises or remain confined to their quarters. It was quite bizarre, but the royal orders could not be flouted for fear of the direst of dire punishments.

The prince was not allowed to step out beyond the palace grounds.

King Shuddhodhan's younger brother Amitodhan had three sons, Mahanama and Anirudh from his first wife, and Anand from his second. They were Siddharth's regular playmates. Then there were other cousins like Devdutt, Baddhiya and Kimbil as well as sons of royal ministers like Udayan, who also gave company to the prince. The general age group was similar, give or take a couple of years.

So, young Siddharth had no dearth of companions to play with within the palace premises. He could not have realized that there was another totally different world beyond the royal walls.

Come to think of it, I also always visited the palace to play with my cousins; they never came out. Of course, I was too young then to notice this, and neither would Siddharth have noticed, or any other child for that matter. If at all, I would have assumed that just as I left my house to visit the palace or the market, those children must be doing the same—if not the local market, then perhaps to visit other cities.

At that age, the only thing that mattered to us was that we were happy being together, playing and eating, having fun and being pampered by the royal servants, who were always there at our beck and call.

I came to know about the story of Siddharth's birth after a few months of our marriage.

It just so happened that I had expressed my wish to go to the market to check out the new fabrics of the season. I knew the merchants visited the city every season, bringing with them new and exotic wares from other parts of the country, especially silk fabrics and threads, beads, sequins and perfumes from Benares. My mother always took me to the market to buy new fabric during these times. The following few months would then be spent in sewing dresses. I was missing it all, and so mentioned it to my mother-in-law.

It was then that I came to know this story and also started to understand my husband a bit better.

'I know the king is very protective, but I always assumed it is because Siddharth is the heir to the throne. I also thought that maybe all princes were raised this way. I never knew that it was connected to his birth chart. How could I have been so unaware?'

'Maybe because people who care for you have been protecting you too, not wanting to upset you with all this. You see, your parents, being our extended family, knew of the prophesies and preventive measures being taken. Come what may, Siddharth has to become the king. And once that happens, all will be fine,' Pajapati sighed deeply.

'Are you saying that Siddharth has never stepped out beyond the palace gates, ever?'

Queen Pajapati nodded her head, and I was shaken to the core by the sheer enormity of the implications of this fact. My poor husband was living a life of lies! I was born and brought up by parents who had taught me to face the truth, yet they themselves had become a part of this charade. It was too much for me to fathom in a day, but then, certain things that I had noticed in my husband's behaviour started making sense. The pieces were falling into place, and I saw the role I was to play in Siddharth's life.

3

GROWING UP

Prince Siddharth grew up in a grand palace of more than three hundred rooms, not including the stores and staff quarters. In contrast, I grew up in a modest mansion of fifty rooms, including the storerooms and staff quarters.

Little Siddharth had thirty-two maids looking after him: eight to feed him, eight to bathe and dress him, eight to play with him, and eight to chaperone him. Queen Pajapati doted on Siddharth, as did King Shuddhodhan. His early years were spent in fun and games. It was pretty much the same for me, except the maids.

We did have a bunch of maids in our house but for cooking, cleaning and other menial jobs, not for looking after me. And I am glad it was so, for I learnt to be self-dependent. My parents saw to it that I did my own chores. When I objected, I was told that to become powerful I needed to understand and harness my own strengths, starting from looking after my own self.

'The real power is within us. It can't be given to us from outside. The outsiders can direct at best, nothing more.'

This message was etched in my heart forever, courtesy my parents.

When I turned six, my formal education started, as was the norm. A tutor would come to our house to teach me the basic subjects. There would be separate masters to teach the crafts like music, dance or painting. It was more or less the same for the royal families like Siddharth's, or families of wealthy merchants and landlords like ours.

Since he was being groomed to become king of the Shakyas, Maharshi Vishwamitra was chosen to teach Siddharth various subjects like languages, economics, arithmetic and ethics. And Acharya Shantidev was chosen to teach him martial arts. The teachers were more than happy as Siddharth was a quick learner. He would learn in a day what others took a week to do. According to both teachers, there seemed a fountain of knowledge deep inside him which just had to be nudged by the right people to flow out.

I felt something similar too, once we were married, but I will come to that later.

The young royal astrologer Kondanna's words haunted the king at all times. Hence, King Shuddhodhan saw to it that his son was surrounded by luxuries. No shadow of sorrow or unhappiness was allowed to come near him.

All of us cousins, close and distant, gathered together regularly at the palace to play. Other than me, there was only one girl called Nandini in our group, but being much younger, she was generally not involved and hung around as part of an audience. I gelled well with the boys and had no qualms in participating in tree-climbing contests or racing around the well-manicured gardens.

Devdutt taught us how to make pipes with tender colocasia leaves and blow through them. We could even sip water through these pipes, but then Devdutt went a step further and taught us to blow seeds through the pipe. Blown hard and swift, the seeds would shoot out at a high speed and could be injurious to anyone coming in their way. The pipe seemed to be more a weapon than a toy to me.

During the seasons of guavas and mangoes, all of us cousins would love to climb the trees to pluck the fruits, which would immediately be taken away to be washed, sliced and served to us by the royal maids.

Out of all the games, the one most loved by the boys was that of holding a court of justice. One of us would be chosen as a leader or a monarch, two would make up a story about some injustice being committed, the remaining would be the courtiers. The leader would have to listen to the story and pronounce their judgement, which would then be opposed by the courtiers. A hot debate would ensue, of course. I had noticed that Devdutt was always quick to pronounce punishment on the offender, whereas Siddharth would get into long-winded discussions, trying to understand why the offender did what they did.

At that time, Siddharth seemed to bore everyone, but later on, much later, I realized that he genuinely wanted to get to the root of the problem, any problem.

I could see that amongst the cousins, Devdutt and Mahanama were closer to each other, as were Siddharth and Anirudh. Anand, the quiet one, generally tried to latch on to Siddharth. On the other hand, Udayan, the son of the chief minister of court, maintained an invisible distance and decorum, though he was treated like a brother by Siddharth.

Sometimes, amidst all this fun and frolic, Siddharth would just get up and walk off on his own. I used to notice that. One day, I followed him to his favourite garden and asked him why he had left the game.

'I am not really into playing games. I can't even hear my own thoughts in all that noise!'

I was amused at Siddharth's answer, as I had no idea that one could hear thoughts. Many years later—after he left us—I recalled those words, as I had started hearing my thoughts then.

Connected to thoughts is yet another interesting episode from Siddharth's childhood. Though I was not a party to it, my mother once told me of an incident at a ploughing festival.

While everyone was busy celebrating the onset of the sowing season with the priests chanting from the scriptures, Siddharth roamed off to one of the farther ends of the palace grounds. Apparently, he sat under a rose-apple tree and became lost in his thoughts.

Afternoon turned into evening, but Siddharth continued sitting the way he was. When the servants found him, they were shocked to see that the shadows of all the trees had shifted according to the direction of the sun's rays, except the one under which Siddharth sat. Word spread like wildfire that Siddharth was a blessed soul, maybe even a god reincarnated. Siddharth was only nine years old then.

This incident led to King Shuddhodhan ordering

three lavish palaces to be built, one each for the summer, winter and rainy seasons. He did not want his son to wander in the gardens. The woods on the periphery of the palace grounds were converted into diligently monitored hunting grounds, beyond which lay denser and more dangerous forests leading up to the equally unfriendly mountains. Siddharth was not fond of hunting, but his cousins and friends were.

Out of the myriad gardens surrounding the palaces, Siddharth was fond of one in particular. This garden had a sizeable lotus pond that remained covered with pink and white lotuses all year round. Sometimes, mostly after rains, blue lotuses could also be seen trying to make space for themselves amidst their pink and white family members. Watching the flowers bloom in different stages was the young prince's favourite pastime.

I knew about it because this was the place he came to when bored of playing with us. That this pond would open my eyes in many ways was something I could not have predicted.

Siddharth had once taken me around the various gardens of the palace under the pretext of playing hide and seek. It was then that he took me to the lotus pond. Frankly, for me, at that age, lotuses were as good as any other flower, so I couldn't share Siddharth's fascination for them.

Later on in life, I realized how these seemingly mundane things that we took for granted had a deeper meaning. The lotus flower had the ability to grow unstained in a murky environment—as did Siddharth.

One day, while young Siddharth was sitting by the

lotus pond, an injured swan fell down from the sky near him. Someone had shot him in the wing with an arrow. Siddharth picked up the injured bird in his arms and gently took out the arrow. Then he rushed to the palace carrying the bird and called for help. Within minutes, the swan was taken care of.

While all this was happening, Siddharth's cousin Devdutt came in. 'That is my bird!' he claimed. 'I shot it while it was flying. I think I have the makings of a great archer,' he gloated with pleasure, more so because he knew Siddharth would never compete with him in this sport.

Siddharth refused to give the swan to his cousin. 'The bird belongs to the sky. You just stopped its flight, that doesn't make it yours. In fact, you tried to kill it, making you its enemy.' As usual, his logic was ready to field any arguments.

'I saved it. So, in case it has to choose whom to go to, I am fairly certain it will come to me, its friend, and not you, its enemy,' Siddharth added further fuel to Devdutt's fire of indignance.

An angry Devdutt stormed to Queen Pajapati with his complaint, hoping to get justice.

Siddharth was adamant. 'I saved the swan's life. Devdutt tried to kill it. The saviour of life should have the right over the life saved, not the taker of life.'

The Queen agreed wholeheartedly with Siddharth, to the acute displeasure of Devdutt. But, as he told me later, Siddharth was not fully satisfied by his mother's judgement that day. Not that the judgement was wrong, but he felt that maybe Pajapati had favoured her son in condoning non-violence rather than understanding the deeper meaning of the entire scenario.

Siddharth, even at that tender age, was full of compassion. It hurt him to see cruelty being done to the weak, or the strong oppressing the powerless.

Devdutt's legendary rivalry with Siddharth went a long way back, the story behind which I came to know subsequently, and will share in due course.

When King Shuddhodhan heard of the swan incident, he was not unhappy, though he was not happy either. He felt that too much compassion was not good for a king; after all, the best of kings were the best of warriors. He discussed the matter with Acharya Shantidev and instructed him to expand his son's curriculum and train him more in warfare.

The king also started inviting Siddharth to attend meetings at the royal court to get him acquainted with political and courtly affairs. The diligent son attended his father's court regularly, but never participated in any of the discussions.

Aware of his son's propensity for debate, Shuddhodhan was expecting some passionate interjections from him. 'Son, you have been attending the court for some time now. I know you must have a number of questions in your mind when you are witnessing our talks. I suggest you start contributing your ideas and sharing your thoughts with everyone. I would like it and so would the others, I am sure.'

'Father, I have realized that the political, economic and military problems that our kingdom keeps facing now and then are rooted in the selfish ambitions of the people who are actually responsible for handling these areas. Since you are dependent on those very people, you can never find solutions to the problems.' Siddharth was not one to mince his words.

This touched a raw nerve as the king recognized the stark truth of his son's viewpoint.

'Son, in order to run a kingdom peacefully like a family, one has to compromise a lot and tolerate even the intolerable members. I am sure once you prepare yourself to run the kingdom, with your talent, you will be able to find ways to purge the system of corruption.'

'It has nothing to do with talent, Father. I believe that one needs to liberate one's own heart and mind first, before trying to resolve the problem. Unfortunately, I am also still trapped in the feelings of anger, jealousy, fear and desire, hence unfit for the role.' This was yet another harsh actuality.

Shuddhodhan could sense the unusual depth of his son's thoughts. It made him proud yet anxious. He could see that such a person would be difficult to tether to a role; he would have to feel free to decide the role he wanted to play.

The king didn't want to lose his son, hence he continued trying to entice him into his own corporeal world. He went on to provide all kinds of distractions for Siddharth as he headed towards adolescence, since it was the right time to learn about carnal and worldly pleasures. Little did Shuddhodhan know that his son had a very short attention span for these kinds of things. All the distractions that were provided for the prince were used and enjoyed to the hilt by his cousins and friends.

As we grew up, Siddharth and I lost touch. I had stopped going to the palace, and to tell the truth, I didn't miss any of it. Our neighbours had two daughters, Kanta and Nirmala. They were my friends. Their father was also a landlord, and their mother was a friend of my mother. We visited each other's houses often.

Kanta was older than me and Nirmala younger. We loved to create things together, like jewellery from flowers, leaves and seeds. Or we would craft boxes, bowls and baskets from tender bamboos or even straw, and colour them with crushed flower petals. We also made windmills with palm leaves that would actually rotate on a windy day.

Sometimes, we would climb trees to pluck fruits, but ate them sitting there on the branches. No fancy maid service for us! We would compete with each other on how many fruits one could eat and how fast, and many a night, I suffered from stomach gripes because of it.

We also played *parihaar patham* by drawing a large circle on the ground, divided into segments, some of which were not to be touched. Then, one of us would throw a pebble from afar into the circle. Moving clockwise, this person would then have to retrieve that pebble, hopping on one leg and avoiding all the lines and prohibited segments of the circle.

Kanta was a strong swimmer, so she would take us swimming to the nearby river Rohini. On the way back, we would pick up colourful pebbles from the riverbank for our gardens.

Behind our house was a tall palash tree. It was my mother's favourite. At the base of it, I had built a small shrine of sorts with pebbles, where I pretended that Mother Goddess rested whenever she came to visit us. Every morning and evening, I would place red flowers, either palash or any other from our vast gardens, and request the Goddess to look after us. That was my little temple and my way of praying.

Just before my eleventh birthday, I got my period. Though my mother and grandmother had prepared me for it, it was a very painful experience. I was laid up in bed for three days. It was a first for me because I had never ever been sick enough to be bedridden in the past, though, I admit, it had not been a very long past.

My mother tended to me night and day with warm towels for my never-ending stomach cramps. I drank a special tea made with coriander seeds, cinnamon and rock sugar to help my muscles relax. Special gruels, and broths with ginger and shatavari were prepared for me. I did not leave my room for five days and was pampered like royalty. The last two days were the best, as I got to eat whatever I wanted, whenever I wanted.

At the end of it, when my mother confirmed that this was going to be a monthly occurrence in my life, my first reaction was to ask if I would always be pampered during these days or was it just a one-off thing for couching the shock.

'Maybe not all five, but yes, you will be looked after for three days for sure.'

My body started showing physical changes in the forthcoming months, but mentally I had changed overnight. On being told that henceforth I should refrain from going to the palace to play, I agreed most willingly. My cousins, the boys who had been my playmates for long, suddenly seemed quite juvenile to me. It was as though I had slept a child and woken up a young woman. I told my mother about it.

'It is the truth, darling, you have changed from a child to a young woman overnight. You now have the power to give birth to another human being.' My mother was so matter-of-fact about it.

'Along with any kind of power comes responsibility. So, you must look after yourself well, especially during these three to five days of every month. This is also the reason why it is customary to isolate women who are having their period. Their bodies need rest and nourishment to recover from the loss of blood.' This pragmatic approach of hers to parenting shaped me to become what I am today.

I remember clearly how strangely empowered I had felt then. It was a kind of superiority, a kind of goddess-like feeling. I felt one with Mother Goddess then. I believe my walk also changed somewhat, bordering on a swagger, at least for some months.

Kanta and I shared a bond now, as she had already gone through all of it and helped me in understanding a few things.

As far as the boys were concerned, I felt that all my cousins back at the palace were such immature kids. Except Siddharth of course. He was different. For the others, I developed a sort of disdain. This phase also lasted for barely a year.

I guess we get bored with our emotions too, especially

the ones that we cultivate, the ones that are superficial and circumstantial, with no real foundation.

My life changed after getting my period; it became quite busy. My mother taught me all about herbs and their use in treating minor ailments. I learnt cooking and about preserving fruits and vegetables through pickling and drying, though I was not fond of cooking much. I always felt that it was too labour-intensive and did not yield appropriate appreciation from the consumers.

I didn't mind sewing or knitting or even embroidery. They were such clean crafts, as opposed to pottery, which was more popular those days. My mother laughed at my choices. 'You were born to be a princess,' she would say often.

I picked up the principles of farming and gardening from my father. Together we dug out a small space behind our house, where I grew herbs, flowers and plants of my choice. I tended to them as one would look after one's pets.

I also learnt how to chisel out little figures from wood, from my father, who I always felt would have made a great carpenter. Later on in life, I was delighted to see my son exhibiting the wood-crafting skills of his maternal grandfather.

My father would also craft small musical instruments with dried gourd, wood and clay pots. All of us in the family loved to sing and dance at the slightest of excuse.

Music was something that Siddharth loved too, his favourite instrument being the flute. 'Notes have to be in the right order for the melody to come through, otherwise it's all noise,' he would say. His way of looking at anything was so unique and meaningful. I learnt much from him in our thirteen years together...and more when he left.

Siddharth taught me to ponder, to question, and not to accept anything blindly. Fortunately, I was already predisposed towards questioning, though it did make me seem obstinate at times.

Coming back to my growing-up years, my best memories are of the stories that my grandmother told me. My maternal grandparents lived far away, with my mother's elder brother. My paternal grandfather had died long ago, and my grandmother lived with her sister in the neighbouring kingdom of Kosal. She visited us every three months or so. I looked forward to those visits as they brought me wonderful stories.

Grandma's stories were about gods and demons, humans and animals, and even plants. My personal favourite was about Kali, the goddess who went around tirelessly killing demons; she was dark yet beautiful, a protector, and the embodiment of female power. According to my grandmother, every woman has a Kali in her, hidden deep inside. I believed her.

'God forbid, if you ever face any trouble in life, do not seek help from anyone, not even family; seek instead from your own self, your own Kali within. She is your hidden power. With her help, you can overcome the toughest of hurdles in life.'

Grandmother's words did help me fight my battles in life, later.

One incident from those times still remains fresh in my mind, as though it had happened just yesterday.

I remember being particularly pleased with myself, as I awaited my grandmother's visit that summer. My tutor had told me the story of Prince Ram of Ayodhya, and how he had won the battle against evil Ravan. I wanted to narrate this story to Grandmother. It was a long story, and I remembered it well. Ram, who went on to become the King of Kosal, was the undisputed hero of all times, and the dream husband for all girls. Marriageable girls were generally blessed by the elders thus: 'May you get a husband like King Ram.'

Coming to my story…all these tales of the victory of good over evil were very popular, but for my grandmother, things were not simply good or bad. She always saw something more than what met the eye.

After listening to my narration of the Ramayan, she asked, 'So why do you think this battle happened between Ram and Ravan? Who started it?'

'Ravan, of course! He kidnapped Ram's wife. The righteous Ram was born to remove all evil from the earth. He killed many demons during his stay in the forest. The evil Ravan was the king of demons. He abducted Ram's wife and took her to his kingdom to make her his queen. Obviously, it was the wrong thing to do, and Ram had to kill him to save his wife. Later on, of course Ram felt sorry for killing Ravan and prayed to God for forgiveness,' I rattled off, almost gloating in triumph.

'This is your tutor's answer, not yours,' Grandma punctured my victory bubble effortlessly. 'Think and tell me. Take your time; we will talk about it tomorrow. Meanwhile, let me check what sweets that old cook of your mother's has made for me.' To say that my grandmother had a sweet tooth would be a gross understatement; her entire denture was sweet, and she practically lived on sweets.

I couldn't sleep that night. Ram was born to destroy evil. Ravan was evil. He had to be destroyed by Ram. The equation was clear in my head. I began to go through the story again in my head.

Ram killed demons like Tadaka, Subahu, Khar, Dushaan, Kabandh, Viradh, Mareech, and many more. Why? Because they were troublesome. Some were not allowing the sages to live peacefully in their hermitages, interrupting their religious rituals, while some demons were actually killing the sages for their food. They were basically indulging in fiendish activities. It was reason enough for Ram to destroy them.

My teenage brain was smitten by Ram, the handsome hero of the Ramayan. He was the epitome of everything that a man should be, and was thus known as Maryada Purushottam, the most righteous, perfect man. So, for me, he was the hero of the story. Since Ram was the hero, the villain naturally had to be Ravan. It was quite black and white really.

My grandmother had a different opinion, as usual.

It was summer time; the sun rose early, and with it rose my grandmother. She would already be out in the herb garden plucking fresh leaves of holy basil for her herbal decoction, when I woke up. She swore by this herbal drink of hers, which she made with about a dozen herbs and spices—including peppercorns, fennel, cumin, cinnamon, cardamom, holy basil, and some other spices that I had never heard of—by boiling them in water for over an hour to get the right potency. The brew thus made was the secret of her health, and her mother's, and her mother's before that, and so on.

Grandma was a treasure-trove of many such magical brews, potions and mixes, which could resolve any physical or mental problems. She was my God, literally a genderless god, as I never saw her as a woman. My mother was a woman, but my grandmother was a person. Maybe this was because my mother was always inclined towards women's causes, whereas my grandmother was neutral and believed in justice for all.

That summer morning, my grandmother sat me down and asked me about the Ramayan. Who or what was the root cause of the battle?

I was firm in my belief that had Ravan not abducted Ram's wife, the battle wouldn't have happened. If Ravan had returned her to Ram, as suggested by his wife and brother, the battle could have been averted for sure. Of course, Ram would still have killed Ravan, as he was duty-bound to kill all demons, but maybe there would have been lesser bloodshed and destruction than what happened because of the battle.

'What is your opinion about Surpanakha?' Grandma asked.

'She was Ravan's sister, a demoness. She tried to entice Ram and Lakshman, but they didn't fall in her trap,' I announced, smug in my knowledge.

'Yes, they didn't fall for her. Instead, they embarrassed her. Ram asked her to approach Lakshman, who sent her back to Ram, and so on. They actually had fun at her expense. Put yourself in her position for a moment and imagine. How humiliating it must be for her to be rejected like this by two men! To make matters worse, Lakshman cut off her nose and ears. I agree that he was short-tempered and was provoked by Surpanakha's attack on Sita. Even then, for a woman to be rebuffed to such an extent!' She paused, looking at me to confirm that I understood the enormity of that incident.

'Surpanakha returned home and told her brother Ravan about the terrible humiliation inflicted on her by the two brothers. Seeing his sister's mutilated face would have made any person's blood boil. In order to avenge that, Ravan decided to hit Ram where it hurt the most. He abducted Ram's wife, and thus launched the battle that forms the core of the Ramayan.'

Ramayan changed for me that day.

I started to see through my grandmother's eyes. I realized that a person should not be judged by their birth circumstances, and that justice should be the same for everyone. Demons are not always evil, nobody is; it's the circumstances that make a person behave in a good or bad, right or wrong manner. That an act should never be seen in isolation was an important life lesson.

At the end of summer, before the onset of the rainy season, we received a royal proclamation. Not just us, it was meant for all the young girls of my age, across the kingdom. We were invited to meet Prince Siddharth formally, as he was declared the Crown Prince.

I wore a light-pink muslin dress with a heavily embroidered

bodice, tapering down to enhance the waist and then flaring just above the hips into a flowy skirt with embroidered motifs scattered all over. I carried a soft pink lace stole with it and somehow managed to tame my then-unruly hair into a bun, precariously hanging on my nape. A dash of kohl in my eyes and I was ready. But my mother was not satisfied. She gave me her own exquisite jewellery to wear, elegant gold bracelets and dainty pearl hoops for my ears.

'I hear that Siddharth will choose his bride today,' my mother mentioned nonchalantly, as we entered the palace gates.

'I don't believe it!' was my knee-jerk reaction. 'How can anyone choose a spouse by just looking at them, as though they were some sort of merchandise?' I wondered out loud.

'This is how brides are chosen in royal families, my dear. They already have the family details of all the eligible girls. The selection does not happen immediately. The prince will make a choice, maybe more than one, and inform his parents. They will confer with the royal astrologers and ministers. After much deliberation, they will reach a verdict and confirm with the prince before informing the girl's parents. It's a long process,' my father explained. Little did he know what lay in store for him, for all of us.

The assembly was in the grand hall. Siddharth was standing on a raised dais with four liveried men, one assisting the girls to step up on the dais to meet the prince, one assisting them to step down after the meeting. One of the men held a scroll from which he read out the introductions of the girls as they approached the prince. The fourth man was overseeing the entire activity.

There was a large gilded box on a pedestal from which Siddharth was randomly taking out jewels and handing them out to the girls after being introduced.

I looked around and saw the girls chattering excitedly, wishing each other luck and wondering who would be the fortunate one, the one who would eventually become the queen of Kapilvastu. It was then that I realized the magnitude of the ceremony, if it could be called so.

The names of the girls were being called one by one. Most of the girls were in awe at meeting Siddharth, and some were wonder-struck by the jewels they received from him. The entire tableaux looked surreal to me and made me want to laugh loudly. It was maybe because I could never be in awe of my childhood friend, as that's what I considered Siddharth to be. And jewels? I was never particularly interested in them anyway.

My name was the last one to be called.

I stepped up on the dais confidently, but the moment I looked at Siddharth, my heart skipped a beat. He looked much older than my last memory of him. Our memory of people and places tends to freeze at our last glimpse of them, doesn't it! It was the same for me. I remembered him from five years ago.

That lanky pre-teen had turned into a tall handsome youth, but his deep brown eyes remained the same. Our eyes met and I blushed, feeling like a woman for the first time in my life. Dressed in yellow silk robes tied at the waist with a bejewelled gold belt, Siddharth looked like how I had imagined Prince Ram to be. I fell in love with him, or maybe I was already in love with him but realized it that day, at that very moment.

Honestly, I didn't know what was happening to me, except that my heart was racing so fast that I was scared it would burst. I felt a tightness in my breast that, be assured, had nothing to do with the dress I was wearing. My hands had become clammy, and I could feel tiny rivulets of perspiration discreetly flowing down my back.

No, I wasn't scared, I wasn't the kind of girl to be scared easily. I was a tad nervous maybe. I wanted Siddharth to feel the same way for me as I did for him, without letting him know or see what I was feeling. A foolish thought, of course, emanating from a love-struck teenager who didn't know that the young man standing in front of her was reading her like a book. Not only that, he was pretty amused by it too, as he told me on our wedding night.

A slight commotion on the dais distracted our attention. It seemed that the box of jewels was empty and Siddharth had nothing to give me.

I felt acutely embarrassed about this mishap, but not Siddharth. Without taking his gaze away from mine, he took off his ring and offered it to me with a smile that increased my nervousness manifold.

'I cannot take this. It would not be right. You can give something to me later…' I started blabbering.

Siddharth gently took my left hand and slid the ring onto my ring finger, while I stood gaping at him, speechless. His tough-looking hands were soft and gentle like rose petals. And his touch was electrifying! However, much as I loved these strange unfamiliar sensations and emotions, I did not want the rest of the people to witness them. I wanted everyone to disappear, or else for myself to escape.

There was a loud cheering from the crowd as my parents rushed to fetch me from the dais. I remained in a dream-like state till I reached home. It was once I changed into my nightclothes that my sanity returned. My mother brought me a cup of warm milk sweetened with honey and sat on my bed as I sipped it.

'The prince putting a ring on your finger has tremendous significance, I hope you know that.'

'I don't know, Mother. I only know that things were different between us today. Something that was hidden for so long, suddenly surfaced. Something connected. Something felt complete. Am I making any sense at all?' I was genuinely perplexed at the turn of events, but was happy, ecstatically so.

I was going through a maze of resplendent possibilities for my future, as though strolling in an enchanted forest under the smiling moon playing hide and seek with the clouds, the fireflies showing me the way. I saw myself as a queen one moment, sitting on an emerald throne, and an angel the next, flying over little houses and sprinkling them with fairy dust. Maybe that's how love spins the hearts and minds of teenage girls.

'Go to sleep, my dear. Tomorrow's dawn will shed light on this.'

And I slept... I slept like a baby that night. I slept a dreamless sleep...maybe because I had entered my own dream.

Early next morning, my father was called to the palace by the King. He returned looking rather pleased with himself, obviously. This was an official meeting between the two fathers, where king Shuddhodhan formally asked my father for my hand in marriage to his son Prince Siddharth. This was the norm of our times, which honoured the girl's father as well as the girl. Giving away his child to another family was considered a huge sacrifice, and the doer was duly respected for that.

The time after that moment, and until I got married, flew by in a blur.

There was much excitement all around me: fittings, rituals, and also training in royal etiquette. Visitors were dropping by…congratulating me and my family… I was to become a princess, subsequently the queen of Kapilvastu, and my son would be king…and so on.

In order to get away from all that chatter, I had devised a place within myself where I loved drowning in my own thoughts and dreams.

Siddharth used to find refuge from the world in the lotus pond of his favourite garden; my lotus pond was inside my heart.

Later in life, Siddharth had to leave his family and home to seek refuge elsewhere, while I stayed within the confines of family and home, as my refuge was within. Some things never change, do they!

This thought amazes and amuses me to this day.

4

TOGETHERNESS

Among the pre-marriage rituals were contests of archery, swordsmanship, horseracing and debate, where Siddharth was to showcase his skills. The idea behind it was to show his worthiness for becoming a king. I felt it was a waste of time, but my mother told me that it was my father's idea.

I was too wrapped up in the throes of my own tumultuous feelings to think about or question anything.

It was many years later that I came to know that my father, being the king's brother-in-law, knew of the prophecy made at Siddharth's birth. Both the fathers wanted to prove it to themselves, more than the rest of the world, that Siddharth was capable of becoming the king of Shakyas. Maybe they also thought that the entire exercise might lure him towards kingship soon. Little did they know that the prince could see through all ploys and was merely amused by them.

Unlike my parents and in-laws, my vision of the future was limited to becoming Siddharth's wife. All the times that I had met him or played with him and his cousins,

I always nursed a soft corner for him. Unlike his cousins or friends, Siddharth was not bossy or boisterous. He was not interested in rough, physically strenuous games. He preferred to play his flute or go for long walks around the vast palace grounds and gardens.

Siddharth's music teacher had gifted him a flute, which he treasured above all treasures. He made his own songs... lyrics, music, the works. Out of his cousins, only Anirudh understood and appreciated music, so it was with him that Siddharth would play his flute.

I always felt that Siddharth was more interested in nature than people; that people are but a part of nature was an understanding that came to me later.

Another impression I had about Siddharth was that he did what his parents told him to do. I could not see him disobeying or answering back, or rebelling against his parents, though he later proved me wrong in this aspect.

His giving me his ring, choosing me as his bride in front of everyone, was probably as unexpected for his parents as it was for me, and perhaps it was more so for them. It was as though he was waiting for me, as though he had already decided to marry me, as though he knew that I was waiting for him too.

It should have been the first red flag for me. It should have shown me that Siddharth actually did what his heart told him to, oblivious to the rest of the world.

That fateful day when Siddharth had looked at me, I had been completely swept off my feet. When our eyes met, it felt like we had known each other since forever, it felt like coming home. For lack of any other suitable word,

I was labelling this feeling of mine as love. Yet, was it what poets defined as love? I didn't know.

Love is blind, they say, but I was not blinded by this emotion. In fact, I could see more clearly. I could see into his depth. I could actually read Siddharth's soul. That is true even today. But in my youth, I did become blinded by my own desires, which I wrongly attributed to love then.

Our marriage was a swirl of colours—vermillion red and turmeric yellow, a profusion of marigolds and red roses, shehnai music, the Vedic chants of 108 Brahmins, the aroma of freshly prepared food mingling with the varied fragrances worn by the guests, the tinkling of jewellery, and the chattering and laughing of people—a grand celebration of happiness.

It was the next largest event after King Shuddhodhan's own first wedding. The entire kingdom was celebrating it by decorating and lighting up their homes.

The wedding ceremony was conducted in the royal temple, the same place where Siddharth and I had first met as babies. It was decorated with marigolds and red hibiscus flowers, and rice flour patterns adorned the floor on which we walked up to approach the deity.

The Mother Goddess looked resplendent in a red robe with gold trimmings. With large life-like, kohl-lined eyes beneath the vermillion-smeared forehead, ornate gold earrings dangling from her ears, a diamond stud adorning her nose, her full red lips parting in a benign smile, the hennaed palm of her heavily bangled right hand raised in blessing—the Goddess set my trepidation to rest. I even had a fleeting cheeky thought that the Mother Goddess somehow reflected me that day, as we were pretty much dressed alike!

Our wedding procession moved from the temple towards the palace, and I was overwhelmed to see the crowd, singing, dancing and showering flower petals on us. As we neared the palace, trumpets heralded our arrival and people started chanting, 'Long live the Crown Prince! Long live Princess Yashodara Devi!'

It was the beginning of my new life, a resounding beginning. Today, as I watched my husband approaching the palace, I felt somewhat the same. It was also the beginning of my new life, albeit a silent one this time.

My journey with Siddharth started on our wedding night, as we discovered each other. He was a little clumsy and shy at first, but together we made magic. We explored each other, and then explored our surroundings together. We went around touring the palaces, the numerous interconnected gardens, and even the groves at the periphery of the palace grounds.

I had already been to one of the great halls of the main palace, the smaller or minor one, for that life-changing event when Siddharth put a ring on my finger in his 'selection of wife' event, but now, after having married him, it was fun to revisit the hall and relive that moment. Then there was the actual great hall, for holding important events wherein visitors or dignitaries from other kingdoms were received by the king.

Besides these, there were a dozen state rooms for royal guests, and a dozen more for the informal meetings of the ministers. Then there were fifty-two royal suites, comprising five rooms each, and twenty leisure rooms. The kitchen area was like a maze of rooms in itself. To top it all, there were secret passages connecting the king's rooms to the various state rooms.

Overall, I could safely say that there was no way I would ever see the entire palace in my lifetime. The smaller three seasonal palaces were less than half the size of the main palace, easily navigable and hence explorable. Mostly we spent the extremes of seasons in them. Siddharth's favourite was the breezy summer palace with its high-roofed rooms and wide open corridors, surrounded by lots of shady trees.

Siddharth showed me his favourite rose-apple tree, the peacock garden, and other nooks and places where he would escape to from the humdrum of royal life. The only strange thing was that we never seemed to go very far. The huge boundary walls beyond the palace grounds outlined the limits of Siddharth's world, and my new world.

Contrary to my expectations, little was expected of Siddharth or me, except for joining the family for occasional meals. Days rolled into weeks, and weeks into months. We were happy—everyone was happy.

My cousins, childhood friends, and playmates were all grown up now. Initially it was a bit awkward talking to them within the prescribed protocol. Eventually, we all got used to it. Just as they treated Crown Prince Siddharth, they treated me with equal respect due to my being a princess. Mahanama, Anirudh, Anand, Baddhiya and Kimbil joined us for meals frequently, but Devdutt was almost always busy elsewhere.

I slipped into my role rather effortlessly, I felt, patting my own back in self-appreciation.

Then one day, I expressed my desire to visit the market…and my world turned upside down on learning how my husband was a prisoner in his own house.

My mother-in-law told me about the prophecy declared at Siddharth's birth, and that the king hoped marriage would help anchor his son to his familial duties. According to King Shuddhodhan, pain and suffering led a person to become religious. Hence, he kept his son away from seeing or experiencing any form of pain or suffering. Now I was expected to take over that role from his father.

I disagreed vehemently, but only within my heart. After all, how could one appreciate pleasure without experiencing pain! They coexisted as two sides of a coin, except the royal family insisted on seeing only one side of it. However, like a dutiful daughter-in-law, I did not argue, but decided to set things right my own way.

Time, or rather life, had fallen into a regimented pattern. By now, I could sense that my love was not enough for Siddharth. He needed something more, at a different level. I also recognized the fact that *I* could not give that 'something' to him, but I could certainly help him get it.

I felt then as I feel now that our bond was of many lives, that I was always with him. I would be with him in this life too…if not in body, surely in spirit.

I started telling Siddharth about life beyond the palace grounds, beyond the boundary walls. I told him about my childhood, my friends other than the ones in the palace, the stories my grandmother had told me, and the discussions

I had had with her about those stories. I helped him see and feel the unseen.

We would go to the farthest garden and sit under the trees to talk. It was like watching a bud opening up ever so gingerly. One day, Siddharth told me about the incident at the rose-apple tree, the one my mother had mentioned long back. Coming from him, the incident appeared completely different.

'I was young, about nine. It was the day of the first ploughing of the year, and, as you know, it is celebrated with much fanfare and feasting. After the prayers for a healthy harvest, my father does the customary ploughing and the festivities begin. That had been the routine for years. That year too, the same happened, except that this time I asked my mother why the scriptures had to be chanted for so long. She told me that the Brahmins were chanting the Vedas that contained profound knowledge. Through the chants, they requested the gods to bless the earth with a bountiful harvest, so that none in the kingdom would remain hungry.

'The heat was increasing and so was my boredom with the never-ending drone of chants. As soon as the prayers were concluded, King Shuddhodhan did the customary ploughing and I slipped away to see actual farmers doing the actual ploughing.

'In one of our fields, I observed a farmer, naked to the waist, prodding his oxen to plough the land. It was getting close to noon, and the man was sweating profusely. Walking up and down the field, intermittently whipping the reluctant oxen making the furrows, the man started looking tired after a while. The oxen had to pull very hard with the wooden yoke upon their necks, their hooves gripping the earth beneath, while their large bodies inched forward, dragging the heavy iron plough behind them to dig the furrows…' Siddharth paused, as though reliving the moment.

'I went closer to observe the furrows. The plough had turned up the soil, exposing the worms that had their homes there. The worms wriggled in distress, trying desperately to find cover. Some of the worms had even been cut in half. Then I realized why so many small birds were hovering above the freshly furrowed fields. They had come to feast on the worms and other bugs that lay exposed in the fresh furrows. Just then, a huge hawk swooped down and caught one of the small birds, presumably for its lunch.

'Watching them, I could feel the toil of the farmer in the heat of the sun, the struggle of the oxen tied to the plough, the pain of the worms, bugs and the small bird losing their lives so abruptly. I felt their pain and fear, and the unpredictability of life itself. How did all that Vedic chanting help these little creatures? Are we asking the gods to feed our hungry bodies at the cost of killing others? The entire ritual seemed very selfish to me.

'Everyone was busy feasting and didn't even notice me as I quietly walked away from there. Reaching the other end of the palace grounds, I sat in the cool shade of a rose-apple tree to reflect on my observations.'

Siddharth paused again briefly, his face softening at the memory of that day. This was the first time he had opened up his heart like this. I simply sat mesmerized, and honoured of course.

'After some time, I don't know how much, I noticed that my thoughts had subsided. The noise in my head had calmed down. I saw that the man, the oxen, the worms, the bugs and the birds, all had one thing in common. They were tied to the conditions of their lives. The worms and bugs were tied to the condition that they were a source of food for the birds. Likewise, the small bird was bound by the condition that it could fall prey to a larger bird. The oxen had to live in captivity and work for their masters. I also saw that life conditions bring fear and pain at times and enjoyment at others. Like the little bird was enjoying the worms one moment but became the food of a hawk in the next moment.

'I don't know for how long I sat there that day. It was evening when a servant shook me out of that reverie,' Siddharth turned to look at me, his eyes full of tender love.

'And what about all that Vedic chanting that had bothered you?' I couldn't stop myself from asking.

'Oh that? I realized that reciting scriptures didn't help the birds and worms for sure. Till date I have no idea whom it actually helps!'

We had a hearty laugh. I knew then that our physical time together was limited. I also knew that I had to support my husband in his journey, which might lead him away from me, but would take me to him eventually.

Looking northwards, from the terraces of our winter palace, we could see the jagged range of the mountains, beyond which towered the mighty Himalayas. This palace was built on a higher ground than the others to get the best of sunlight. Not only that, we had the best views in the entire kingdom of Kapilvastu from our balconies.

As we would sometimes lie under the starry night sky, Siddharth would look wistfully at the mountains and express his desire to explore them. He was actually fascinated by all aspects of nature—high mountains, deep seas, undulating rivers, thunderous waterfalls, dry deserts, dense forests—and wanted to experience them.

On one such night he told me a story.

'See those mountains, Yasho, behind them are the glorious ranges of the snow-clad Himalayas, the king of mountains. That entire region from there down to the borders of our kingdom is packed with dense forests inhabited by savage animals like tigers, rhinos and elephants. Men venturing to enter that wild region have not returned, I am told. Maybe they were killed by the animals or bitten by poisonous bugs and died, nobody knows.'

Siddharth loved the sight of the mountains more than that of fields. They seemed so unattainable somehow, and probably that was the attraction.

'I have heard a story of a two-headed bird that long ago lived in the mahua trees of the Himalayan forests. The name of one head was Garud and the other Upagarud. The two heads shared all the food that they hunted. Though they ate individually, the food would enter the common stomach, satisfying both of them,' Siddharth started telling me the story, one of many he had heard from his various teachers. Later on, much later, I came to hear more stories from him, and some about him, from Anand and Channa, and even Kisa.

'When this bird wished to sleep, the heads took turns.

One head would keep watch while the other slept. Once it so happened that Upagarud was asleep and Garud was keeping a watch. The mahua tree on which they lived was in full bloom. Fanned by the breeze, the fragrance of the mahua blossoms wafted towards Garud, who was tempted to eat one of them. "If I eat this delicious flower, it will go down into the stomach and Upagarud would also get to enjoy it," thought Garud. Thus, justifying his action, Garud ate the flower.

'Upagarud woke up in the morning happy and satisfied, and wondered what could have led to that feeling. Garud told him of the previous night's incident. Upagarud was angry at having missed out on tasting the delicious flower himself. He decided to do something similar, just to spite Garud.

'Time passed. Once, they happened to alight near a poisonous tree, and Garud went to sleep while Upagarud kept watch. Seeing the fruit of the poisonous tree, Upagarud decided to eat it to teach Garud a lesson.'

'Oh my god! Wouldn't they both die, since they shared the same body?' I was horrified to visualize the consequence.

'Of course, that's what happened eventually. Garud woke up in pain. Upagarud then told him that he ate the poisonous fruit deliberately to make him suffer. See the foolishness! He killed himself too while trying to teaching Garud a lesson.'

'So, what is the moral of the story?'

'The moral is obvious. But I told you the story because I have felt this very strongly many times that in our past I must have been Garud and Devdutt Upagarud.'

Siddharth could be right, as Devdutt had not changed over the years. If at all, he had become overtly competitive and viciously jealous of Siddharth. In fact, he hardly met us after our marriage. We just met at family functions at times, that too not very often. Out of the cousins, Anand and Anirudh spent a lot of time with us.

Meanwhile, I continued telling Siddharth about the marvels of the outside world. I described the various craftspeople, and how they created beautiful things for us as well as how they procured their resources. I told him about weavers and potters and whatever else my parents had taught me about, in addition to all the folktales I had grown up listening to.

Finally, his curiosity was sufficiently piqued, and he sought permission from his father to step out of the royal confines. Surprisingly, this time King Shuddhodhan agreed, albeit reluctantly, and we started going out, exploring the country. It was a momentous step in Siddharth's life, one that would help him understand what he was actually seeking.

As per the king's proclamation, the roads running through the town were prepared for the prince's passing through. The countryside was swept clean, the houses were freshly painted, varicoloured silk curtains hung from the windows, and the people looked happy. The aged and the crippled remained safely inside their homes, out of view of the royal entourage. Yes, we had to travel in an entourage, with criers marching ahead, announcing our passing with drums and gongs. This also ensured that the streets were not defiled in any way.

The general impression was of prosperity and happiness; even the animals seemed happy. And this was true to a great extent. It was common knowledge that since Siddharth's birth, the Shakya kingdom had flourished in every way. There was no dearth of food or money, crops and trade were thriving, and there was an overall feeling of contentment in people.

I understood the king's concern for his son; I was concerned too.

Looking at Siddharth, I could see that he seemed happier, even somewhat satisfied, since we started going out into the real world. Of course it was not really real, but it was more real than the world Siddharth had been living in thus far. It certainly was a step forward in life's journey for him.

Our question–answer game continued. Siddharth had many questions that I loved to answer. He made many observations that he candidly shared with me.

Siddharth observed that the conditions of life were different for everyone. Some led a better existence than others. Even in the case of animals, some like the peacocks of royal gardens enjoyed a greater degree of freedom and safety than others like the oxen. In the case of humans, some were strong while others were weak, some were clever and others foolish, some were beautiful while some were not. Regardless of what conditions they were born in or with, one thing stood out above all else. All living beings wanted to live in peace and happiness. All living beings wanted to avoid suffering.

According to Siddharth, all living things were thus

interconnected with one another through this one universal wish to be happy. He himself was no exception.

Unknown to his parents, Siddharth started going into meditative trances frequently. I would ask him what he saw or felt during those moments. He mentioned abstract things, clouds, wings, light, and a sense of quietude. But I saw more. I saw the call of his soul.

I treasured every moment of our togetherness, this shared bliss, as I knew it was limited. Slowly but surely, I was mentally preparing myself for the inevitable.

A decade passed away thus.

Meanwhile, there was pressure building in the royal family. They were expecting a baby from us. According to the royal astrologers, the triad was as yet incomplete. Duty to domain, wife and child were the three arms of the triad that grounded and sustained a man, the scriptures declared, according to the royal priests.

As was done to resolve any problem, Brahmins were invited from all corners of the kingdom and a fire-sacrifice was held. Prayers were offered to the Mother Goddess to bless us with a child.

Eventually, eighteen months later, I was pregnant.

It was a precious pregnancy, hence Queen Pajapati forbade me to step out of the palace. I told Siddharth to continue his outings. Initially he was reluctant to go alone, as he had developed a kind of dependency on me. Finally, he followed my advice and resumed his trips.

Unknown to both of us at that time, Siddharth was gradually being weaned away from me.

I spent most of my time in my room, caressing my

ever-swelling belly and staring out of the window. As the baby grew within my womb, so did the feeling of impending separation from my husband. I loved them both, but knew that only one would remain with me.

Whenever Siddharth stepped out, my heart would be uneasy till he returned. Though my brain continued to echo that my husband was a responsible, dutiful person and would take care of me and our child, my heart was on its own trip…not in my control at all.

I had deputed Channa, Siddharth's man-servant and stableboy, to be my eyes and ears.

Their first few outings were free from any untoward incident. According to Channa, Siddharth felt so much at peace when out on the road that he would lapse into long silences. Only I knew what those silences were, but I didn't want to dwell on them much.

A day came when Siddharth was rudely shaken out of his trance-like silence by the abrupt stopping of his carriage. They had stopped to allow a very sick man being helped by two men to cross the road.

Siddharth asked Channa about it and was told that the man was very ill, and thus was being helped by his sons. He wanted to know more about being ill, but the only answer he got from Channa was that sickness could strike anyone at any time. Siddharth returned that day confused and saddened.

'What did Channa mean by being ill? Are we all going to be ill one day?' It was difficult for Siddharth to imagine any of his loved ones being ill and helpless like the man he saw. He looked at me with much concern. Then I realized that I did seem to be sick at times due to my pregnancy!

I laughed and assured my husband that pregnancy was not an illness, though yes, anyone could fall sick at any time in their lives. I sat him down and told him about my grandmother and mother, how they healed sicknesses with simple home-grown herbs, and how my grandmother maintained that sickness was just nature's way of telling us that we had gone off-balance. Bringing the balance back almost always set us right. Our bodies are constantly working; even while sleeping, our heart pumps blood continuously, we breathe and we grow. It is akin to a moving carriage—if any one of its wheels as much as cracks, the entire carriage loses its balance.

This seemed to satisfy Siddharth somewhat.

My husband's next outing made him come across an old man; a very shrivelled and bent old man sitting under a tree, barely able to breathe or move. Horrified at the sight, Siddharth turned to Channa for an explanation.

'This, My Prince, is an old man. He was once an infant and then grew to manhood, like you. But now he has come to the end of his days. The years advance and bring us all to this state.'

'Does this fate then await my father, and others?'

'Yes, My Lord, this is the fate of everyone who is born. But do not worry, Sire, you have a long life ahead of you yet.'

Siddharth fell silent. Old age being an inevitability was very difficult to digest for him. I would like to remind here that the sick and the old were not allowed into the palace precincts, so Siddharth was rightly shocked.

On reaching home, he shared his concern with me, and I explained to him by giving the example of a plant growing up to be a huge tree. He began to look at every plant very carefully thereafter. In a way, this entire exercise was very amusing, at least for me, though I could see where it was leading.

Next, Siddharth saw a funeral procession, which was the most difficult situation for him to understand.

'My Master, this is death. This man is no more, his spirit has faded away. His family is taking his body to a cremation ground, where it will be burned to ashes. This is how all of us will end one day,' Channa had explained.

For a person to stop living suddenly, and to then be burnt was incomprehensible to Siddharth, more so when he applied it to his loved ones. He came home looking absolutely shattered. I explained the cycle of life in plants, animals and humans to him. He understood, but wanted to know why. He questioned life's existence and duration. This time, I had no answers.

'About one thing I am convinced—if I want to help others, I need to first find out how to do so. For that, I need to understand the nature of the conditions that create suffering for man; only then will I be able to change them so that everyone is happy. This should be my prime duty as a member of the ruling family,' Siddharth would say.

He began going into his meditative trances more frequently—even when sitting in a song-and-dance *mehfil*, of which there were plenty. King Shuddhodhan had special palaces built for the entertainment of the royal family, as well as harems for male members of the family and their friends. But Siddharth's interest only lay in music, which he loved to compose himself, too.

Interestingly, after his third outing, Siddharth started seeing deeper meaning in the words being sung by the royal singers, and even the courtesans.

'So free, so thoroughly free am I, from three crooked things set free; from mortar, pestle and crooked old spouse…'—to Siddharth would mean that the person was talking about their freedom from desire, which otherwise led to ageing and death.

Not only me, but others in the family too started noticing Siddharth's listlessness. Udayan, son of the chief minister, and Siddharth's childhood friend, tried his best to entice him by parading beautiful women in front of him. Siddharth remained unaffected.

'I have seen sickness and old age. I am certain of death. Nothing can now give me peace of mind. These temptations are all a bunch of lies!' Siddharth's listlessness was now turning into vexation.

He continued having his meals with me, but would go off thereafter. Most of the time, I could hear him pacing the long corridors of the palace. He slept very little and seemed to be waiting for something, maybe a sign of sorts… We did not talk as much, as I could no longer fathom his line of thought and had no satisfactory answers to offer him.

And then, I began to spiral into a world inside of me that I did not even know existed…the dark world of inquietude.

I became afraid of darkness. I ordered all the lamps, and there were many, in my rooms to be lit by sunset. The sight of an unlit lamp would dry up my throat to the point of choking. My stomach would churn painfully and my hands would get clammy. I had entered the realm of fear.

Chronicling those moments makes me shudder even today.

One such dark night, I had a dream, which seemed more like a nightmare to me. I can still recall it vividly.

The earth was shaking, the tallest mountain was swaying, and a savage wind was blowing, uprooting trees and wrecking everything in its way. The sun, the moon and the stars had fallen from the sky onto the earth. I stood naked, stripped of my clothes and ornaments. My hair was cropped short, and I had lost my crown. I was standing next to my bridal bed, which was broken. My husband's royal robes and jewels were scattered on the broken bed. Meteors constantly sped across the sky over the darkened city. Meru, the king of mountains, was trembling.

I woke up crying in terror. Siddharth instantly gathered me in his arms and gently wiped away my tears. I told him about my nightmare. He smiled.

'It is not a nightmare, my dear Yasho, you have dreamed a lovely dream. It is predicting a release for you and me from the forest of desires and the web of passions that have captivated us. It is indicating that I shall bring the light of wisdom to this ignorant blind world. It is a wonderful dream showing that one day you will defeat evil and receive infinite praise; even the gods will bow before you.'

I could not fully believe nor understand my husband's interpretation of my dream, but whatever he said sounded good, and I curled up feeling secure in the support of his arms and fell asleep.

Siddharth's restlessness seemed to be growing at the same rate as my pregnancy. The difference was, his problem pushed him outside the palace while mine pulled me inside.

One day, Siddharth decided not to take the carriage or the horse, but just walk instead. He strolled through the countryside, the green fields calming his senses. The fact that his father kept away the realities of life from him was eating him up from the inside. Since sickness, old age and death were unavoidable, man's self-obsession seemed foolish to him, as did the illusion of strength, of youth, and of life itself. The emotions of joy, grief, hatred, scorn, desire, love, doubt, weariness—they all dropped away from him. Yet, he was not at peace.

Lost in his contemplations, walking aimlessly, Siddharth suddenly spied a monk. Dressed in ochre robes, he was walking peacefully, seemingly far from all the worries of the world. Siddharth saw a ray of hope and felt slightly relaxed, after a long time.

As Siddharth was narrating this incident to me, I felt fairly convinced that to find the answers to his questions, my husband was likely to take a strong step—a step I was dreading. We made love…and as I touched his face with my trembling fingers, suddenly we both realized our impending separation…and broke into silent tears.

Things moved very fast from then on, for both of us.

My fears increased. The thing about fear is that it does not exist in the present; it needs the past or future to feed on, like a feedback loop, to keep it alive. Rooted in a story of a prophecy from the past, my fear had jumped into my future, enveloping my present in its blackness.

The situation was getting out of control—out of my control, that is.

Apparently Siddharth had reached a decision in his mind, and he met his father the next morning.

'Dear father, I would like to seek the path to deliverance, for which I must leave the palace. I am looking for the answer to pain, to suffering, and I am unable to find it while living here.'

King Shuddhodhan was naturally and understandably shocked. 'Son, you are too young to think like this. In fact, it is time that I leave the palace, handing over the throne to you. Savour the joys of fatherhood, the challenge of ruling a kingdom, before you think of seeking anything for yourself. At this time, your wife, your family and your subjects need you more than you need yourself.'

'Promise me four things and I shall drop the idea of leaving.'

The king felt a tad hopeful, though the feeling was short-lived.

'Promise me that I will never grow old, that my life will not end in death, that sickness will not impair my health, and that my fortune will remain as it is right now.'

'How is this even possible! You must stop thinking on these lines and get back to your responsibilities first.' The king was obviously annoyed.

'Since you cannot promise me these four things, please do not hold me back, Father. It's a troubled world we live in; I want to bring peace to everyone. I want to find an alternative to suffering. I want to remove the darkness that hides the light of wisdom, and I want to find out how to do that. I am sorry, but I have to leave.'

Having informed his father of his decision, Siddharth must have felt somewhat relieved. At least that was the impression the king had, as conveyed to me after the news of his son's leaving broke out the next day.

Unfortunately, Siddharth could not gather enough courage to tell me, his wife, of his decision—a life-altering decision for me and our baby.

That fateful evening, when the moon was eclipsed, our son was born.

Actually, I was scheduled to deliver a month prior, according to the royal midwife. She had been fretting over me for the past nearly two months, examining me and announcing that the baby was fully formed and ready to come—only that it didn't. I had started feeling the baby's kick in my belly soon after the fourth month into my pregnancy, which was much earlier than normal, according to the midwife. Based on that, she had declared the baby to be a boy, a prince eager to be out in order to survey his kingdom!

Unfortunately, the baby didn't seem to want to come out at all.

The evening when I finally delivered, it still seemed that the baby was unwilling to be born. The paroxysms of pain were wrecking me, yet the childbirth was not progressing. The midwife had to use warm herbal poultices to induce labour. I could feel the baby clinging to the silken walls of my womb. Why was it so scared to come out? Were my fears of losing my husband affecting my baby too?

As this thought flashed through my mind, I was overwhelmed with guilt.

I prayed to Mother Goddess for forgiveness and vowed to love and protect my baby to the best of my ability, till my death. Then I requested the baby to let go of me and to come out into this beautiful world, where I promised to look after him forever. It worked. The midwife cried in excitement, as I did in agony. The baby was moving. It had decided to enter the world, my world.

Little did I know that seven years later I would be telling my heart to let go of the same baby, for him to enter into yet another world—his father's world this time.

During those excruciatingly painful hours of delivery, losing blood and slipping in and out of consciousness, I had obliterated Siddharth from my thoughts. I realized that to do justice to both, only one could be in the scabbard of my mind. Retrospectively, I feel that it was nature guiding me to hold on to the one who needed me most, at that time.

I also believe that in seeing the beginning of life, which he had now produced, Siddharth must have again begun to question the meaning of life's existence and duration. This must have catalyzed his departure.

As I lay exhausted after delivering our son, I sensed Siddharth peeping into our room, before walking away into the night. He did not come in. Maybe he thought we were sleeping peacefully—my baby was, but I wasn't. I turned just in time to see my husband turning away. The baby whimpered, as though pulling me back to reality. I tended to him immediately, tears of anguish blurring away my happiness of bearing him.

Today the situation is similar. My anguish overshadows my happiness. I know I will lose my son, even as I get to meet my husband after seven years. But then, there is a difference…it was a dark moonless night then, it is a bright sunny day today.

5

ABANDONMENT

Though I did have nightmares that indicated my husband's abandoning me in some way or the other, I was always in denial. My logic would kick in, and I would tell myself that Siddharth could leave me any time, assuming I would understand his needs, but he wouldn't do that to his child. He was a dutiful father, wasn't he! He would know that the child didn't ask to be born; we brought it into this world, and hence we were responsible…

I had all kinds of reasons ready to explain why he wouldn't or shouldn't abandon us, but I guess his reasons were stronger.

So, even when I sensed Siddharth was leaving that night, I went into my customary self-protective mode of denial. Childbirth had taken a physical toll on me, and I drifted into a fatigued stupor. In fact, I ignored the night as one of my nightmares. Retrospectively, I have wondered many times, could I have stopped my husband from abandoning us? Did I unknowingly manifest what I was dreading all the time?

Was it what my grandmother used to say all the time, that our thoughts create our reality? She would tell all of us, even the maids sometimes, that we should not only speak good but also think good. She would say that everything, all creation, including us, are god's thoughts, and that we can also create for us the life that we want by thinking about it sincerely. Honestly, this sounded like some magic hocus-pocus kind of fantasy of hers at the time.

Little did I know then, that grandma's words were never said in vain. The dreaded thought of Siddharth leaving consumed me for years…and maybe got manifested.

I always prided myself on being sensible and strong, a free spirit. I knew I could be mulish at times, maybe a bit short-tempered at others, but I still managed thirteen years of marriage without losing my sanity…up until that morning.

I woke up to the protective chanting of Brahmins and the overpowering fragrance of incense they were burning in lamps as part of the week-long post-delivery cleansing ritual.

The first person I saw in the dimly lit room was Channa, and I knew that the night before had been no nightmare. It was true. It had happened. My husband had left us—his wife and newborn son.

Channa, Siddharth's trusted man-servant, and companion since childhood, stood before me looking deathly pale and trembling uncontrollably. Handing me my husband's rings and a lock of hair, he collapsed on the floor and broke down.

'Please forgive me, My Lady, I could not stop him!'

'Shush...stop crying and tell me what happened.' My irritation was mounting. I had no patience for his tears.

'Sire woke me up at midnight and asked me to saddle up and fetch his horse Kanthak. I did as told. We rode into the night, out of the eastern gates of the palace. Riding fast, piercing the cold darkness of the night, we were out of the Shakya kingdom in no time. But Master did not pause there. He rode on, and I followed. After a long time, after crossing many *yojana*s, crossing the kingdom of Koliya, we reached the banks of the river Anoma. Beyond the river lay the dense forests of Magadh.

'Following the river downstream, we managed to find a shallow place to cross it on our horses. After crossing the river, we continued to ride a bit more. Finally, dismounting near the forest, the prince cut off his hair with his sword. Then he gave the jewels and hair to me to be handed over to Your Highness, and the sword to be handed over to His Majesty, King Shuddhodhan.

'At that moment, we saw a hermit passing by. The prince stopped him and exchanged his royal clothes with the man's rough ones. Wearing the hermit's robes, he told me to return with Kanthak. "Tell my father, what he tried to prevent me from seeing is what I now go to seek. Tell my wife I will return only once I have conquered old age and death. Do not follow me!" He ordered, and went off into the forest.' Channa continued to sob inconsolably.

'I cried and begged him to change his mind, for the sake of his newborn son at least if not anyone else, but he just smiled and asked me return fast and reach the palace by daybreak.'

Rohini entered the room just as Channa left. His words were like hot lava being poured into my ears. For a moment I went blank. Then, all at once, it registered in my brain. Siddharth was gone! All the blood seemed to drain away from my body. I was numb. It was as though my entire world had just crumbled in front of me, as though all the doors had shut on me, as though the earth beneath me had turned into air…it was unreal.

I screamed.

Queen Pajapati came rushing to my room and embraced me, holding me close to her bosom. Rohini took away the baby to the nursery, while we two grieving women cried our hearts out—my pent-up tears of thirteen years, my mother-in-law's of twenty-nine years. After what seemed like an eternity, we sat on the bed exhausted. I narrated all that Channa had told me to my mother-in-law, handing over the hair and jewels to her.

Looking into the wise old eyes of Queen Pajapati, I saw the depth of her grief. She must have gone through a similar hell when twenty-nine years ago her sister Queen Maya passed away, leaving her week-old baby in her arms. To make matters worse, she was married to her sister's husband, who, immersed in his own painful loss, couldn't be bothered about her existence.

How Pajapati must have coped with the simultaneous anguish of the death of a loved one and the call to life by the newborn one! And now, she was faced by yet another devastating loss, the loss of her son. However, behind all that grief, her eyes were brimming with compassion. I suddenly felt very insignificant.

After my sobs somewhat subsided, the Queen held me at an arm's length and said, 'Siddharth has left to find his way through suffering. You must do the same here, now. Your son needs you, as Siddharth needed me then. And as I found my way, you will also find yours.'

Her words struck a familiar chord. Siddharth used to say that it was suffering that united us. That day, I had suffered the loss of a loved one for the first time in my life. I came to understand what suffering meant. I also understood and felt my mother-in-law's suffering, just like my husband felt the suffering of that farmer, his oxen, the worms and the birds.

I realized an important truth that day—unless we learnt to be with suffering, be with ourselves and others in suffering, we could not be free of suffering, though freedom from suffering was not even on the horizon yet. Realizing the truth was one thing, and living it was another, as I would understand over the next two years.

Every time I was alone, I would ask myself, why did Siddharth walk away? Our togetherness had always seemed timeless to me, as though our souls had been threaded together since many lifetimes before. Wrapped up in my thoughts, I started neglecting my baby, forgetting to nurse him.

As for my thoughts, they were more like noise. There was a cacophony of loud cries, mad laughter, angry ravings, incessant sobs, rumbling thunder clouds, crackling lightning, and harsh rains, all overlapping each other and interspersed with people talking incoherently in my head. This noise remained in my head at all times, varying in intensity and content once in a while, but nevertheless it was there all through, blurring the lines between days and nights.

My body did not feel as though it had brought forth another human being into this world, at least not to me from inside. My milk started drying up. The royal wet nurses were at the beck and call of the baby. I suppose royalty has its own perks, which can come quite handy at times.

Whenever I sat in my room, which was most of the time, I would stare at the door, wishing it would open and Siddharth would walk in—the Siddharth I married, the vulnerable yet strong man I fell in love with. Often, I would get so lost in the door that I would become oblivious to my baby's cries. Rohini or some other maidservant would then rush in to pick up and pacify the baby. Eventually they stopped bringing him to my room at all.

Gradually, my body refused to move of its own accord. I wanted to remain lost in my own isolation. The cleansing chants, instead of helping, seemed to intensify my agony.

A week later, after the cleansing was over, my mother came to spend time with me. She hadn't visited me in the past few years, since the time she fell sick. It was not really sickness that she had but old age creeping up fast on her. She had had a back injury in her youth, which had flared up and led to a cascading effect of other joints becoming affected, resulting in diminished mobility.

Considering that sick and old people were banned from entering the palace premises, my mother could not come to visit us for a long time. After Siddharth's departure, the rules were relaxed. In any case, those rules couldn't do much to prevent him, could they!

My mother said nothing to me, asked nothing; she just enveloped me in her love. She looked after me as she did when I was little, bathing me, dressing me, combing my hair, feeding me and sleeping next to me, caressing my hair till I fell asleep.

She brewed special herbal decoctions for me using roots of turmeric and ginger, fennel seeds, cinnamon, cardamom and clove, which she would feed me with a spoon, like a baby.

I was reminded of my grandmother's stories.

When the gods and demons churned the ocean of milk in search of ambrosia, the nectar of immortality, the first thing to come out was poison and then turmeric, and finally ambrosia. Ginger was a favourite healing root used by Charak, the healer of the ancients. He called it the root of wisdom. Fennel was consumed by Sage Vasishta after he swallowed the demon Illwal, so he would not come back to life again.

Once guarded by snakes in the deep recesses of the earth, cinnamon was burnt by kings to atone for their sins. Cardamom, also called the herb from the planet Mangal, offered effective magical protection, and was used as a love charm by the celestial dancers and nymphs. Associated with Lord Shiva and Hanuman, cloves have been offered in fire sacrifice since ancient times, to ward off illnesses and resolve all obstacles in life.

These were some of the stories I remembered, and these transported me back to the carefree days of my childhood.

I started relaxing—that is to say, my body started relaxing. The herbs healed my womb and strengthened my muscles. I could move my limbs now and slowly started moving around a bit in my room.

One morning, my mother brought my baby to me, and seeing his cherubic face with big innocent eyes wrung my heart and made me feel so helpless. The dam in me burst. Giving the baby to the maid to be taken away to the nursery, my mother held me close, as my tears flowed in rivulets down her back.

'I am sorry he left, my child. Whatever his reasons might be, they have nothing to do with you. Never ever blame yourself.'

The word 'blame' triggered something in me. I sat up. Was I really blaming myself in some way, maybe unconsciously? That I couldn't hold him back, that I couldn't make him change his mind, that I couldn't answer all his questions…

Yes, I was blaming myself. I felt inadequate. I felt I could not complete him as he did me.

Siddharth was a rational, cerebral person, uninterested in material pursuits, which left me no space to question my physical attributes, or the lack of them. His hunger, his needs were different, and that's where I felt guilty of not being able to satisfy him. My dissatisfied husband was hence compelled to abandon me and seek satisfaction elsewhere. Mental or emotional rejection is as heartbreaking as physical rejection, or maybe more, as it is intangible and difficult to comprehend and rectify.

'He didn't leave because of me, but neither did he stay back because of me. What must people be thinking! My husband abandoned me. I feel so betrayed, somehow.' I was angry at my husband as well as myself—mainly myself for not being able to cope.

My mother looked at me tenderly and said, 'This sadness will go away, it always does. Every new mother goes through a flood of emotions because her body is adjusting to so many things that have happened inside her. Creating and giving birth to a life is no mean task. That is why, traditionally, new mothers are kept in confinement for forty days.'

'It is not sadness, Mother! It is much more than that. My body may have been ripped open by the baby, like yours and of many others before me, so I understand all that. It will take its time to heal. But what about my heart? It has been ripped apart by my husband abandoning me. That I don't understand. How many new mothers do you know who have gone through this?'

I could not bear to be compared with other women, as I felt mine was the rarest of rare cases. After all, what father would leave his wife and newborn baby without as much as a word of explanation or even saying farewell! It was not normal. My situation was not normal. I refused to be convinced otherwise.

'Sadness is an emotion, darling. Its cause can be any and many. And every sad person feels that their sadness is special.' Well, my mother was nothing if not forthright in putting her point across. 'Your pain is deep, I understand that. It is scaring you. It has made you intensely sad. It has turned you away from your own self and even your son. Your body will heal itself in some weeks, but who will heal your heart? You have to do it yourself.'

My mother held my hands and continued, 'Because if you don't, this sadness will engulf you and destroy you and your baby. Any emotion is powerful only till the time we make it so. And any emotion has the tendency to become powerful when we are at our most vulnerable, which is where you are at now.'

'What is the solution then?'

'You have to heal yourself. You have to close what has been opened, one stitch, one step at a time, just like you mend a torn garment or a broken toy. I told you once that our power is within us…do not let it leak away! Fix the leak.'

'I don't know how…' I understood what my mother was trying to explain to me, but continued feeling helpless.

'We will start by spending more time with your baby.'

Things became a shade better after that, but just a shade, not more. My body was recovering gradually, and I was able to nurse my baby, though not as much as the baby desired. I had started eating better and sleeping better.

And so came the day of naming my eleven-day-old son, in the same temple where Siddharth and I were named twenty-nine years ago.

I was not up to it, but my mother and mother-in-law were there as my support system for this very important ritual. The event was celebrated with much singing, dancing and feasting. King Shuddhodhan probably wanted to show his people that he was unaffected by his son's leaving.

The priest conducted a fire ritual, and after studying the planetary positions at the time of my baby's birth, declared his name as Rahul. I was taken aback, because the planet Rahu was a shadow planet according to astrology, and the time of day under this planet's influence was considered inauspicious.

'Wouldn't it be an inauspicious name?'

'Princess, your son was born during a lunar eclipse, in the shadow of the planet Rahu. We have to respect the planetary deity, keeping in mind the power of Rahu's wrath.' The priest was firm about the name.

I wasn't convinced, nor was I pleased. But then, I was too weak in body and spirit to discuss the matter any further.

My mother-in-law took the baby from me, and kissing his forehead said, 'Any name has more than one meaning, but for me, a name has no meaning.'

She hugged her grandchild, eyes glistening with unshed tears. I am sure she must have been re-living a similar moment from twenty-nine years ago, when Siddharth was named. It was true; what did names matter anyway!

The day's exertion had exhausted me completely. My mother kept my baby away from me and treated me like a baby instead. Making me sip her herbal concoctions every couple of hours and massaging my feet with aromatic oils, she was there like my shadow. I don't recall for how many hours I was awake or asleep during those couple of weeks; time flew past in a haze.

More than a month passed, my mother's ministrations had borne fruit—I was regaining my strength. As always, she was right; my body had healed by the end of six weeks. I was able to spend more time with my baby, to the immense satisfaction of his two doting grandmothers.

I started stepping out of my rooms and taking walks in

the gardens. Often I would be accompanied by my mother. One such late afternoon, we walked beyond the lawns and sat on a bench under the shade of kadamb trees. The patch where the trees grew was landscaped as a small hillock, and one got a beautiful view of the sprawling colourful gardens from up there.

Admiring the profusion of nature's colours while resting my head on my mother's shoulders, I felt like a child again—the little girl who used to visit and play in these gardens what seemed like centuries ago.

'Look at the amazing colours all around us, Mother… such beautifully crafted flowers dancing in the sun…'

'Look at these little flowers too, enjoying the shade,' she pointed at some small pretty white flowers under the trees. 'Do you remember our herb garden, back at home, dear?' As I nodded, she continued, 'Some plants need sunlight to grow, while others thrive better in shadows. We have a patch of medicinal herbs growing in shade—powerful herbs like Brahmi.'

In her inimitable way, my mother was telling me not to worry about my son being born in the shadow of Rahu. Mothers sense everything, even the deepest of secrets about their children, don't they? I sat up and hugged my mother with renewed energy, much to her amusement.

A mother is like god—no wonder we worshipped Mother Goddess and addressed earth as mother. I felt blessed to be a mother.

All this while, I had felt that had I not been pregnant, I could have accompanied my husband, like Sita accompanied Ram. That afternoon, I realized what my mother meant when she had said that women have power in their wombs—we do, we create life in our wombs, and with that one act, we get closer to God; we become gods!

When this realization dawned, my eyes started seeing beyond my own self. I saw how frail my mother had become physically. She had aged at double the speed in the last thirteen years since my marriage. I could see her collarbones through her robes, and her eyes had sunk deeper. Her walk had become laboured because of her stiff back and painful knees. Yet, she had put every pain aside to look after me. I suddenly felt overwhelmed.

'Mother, you have stayed long enough with me. Now I think you should go back home and take rest. As you can see, I am pretty much on the road to recovery.'

'No darling, I intend to stay till the feeding ceremony of my grandson.'

She brushed aside my concern. Little did I know then why she wanted to spend so much time with me and my baby…

As the months passed, Rahul kept growing fast. He could sense me visiting the nursery and turned his little head to look at me. He would smile and gurgle at me, as though trying to say something. He had even started rolling over in his crib and actively threw about his pudgy arms and legs. A happy and friendly baby, Rahul soon became everyone's darling. His grandfather and both grandmothers doted on him, as did his nursemaids. Seeing so much love being showered on my son, I was certainly happy, but mostly, I felt more like an onlooker than a participant.

Baby Rahul was getting stronger. Now he could be

propped up on pillows, though not for long, as he would invariably tumble off onto the side in his excitement. Soon he would start teething, and a day would be decided to hold his feeding ceremony.

Once Rahul crossed his fifth month, the royal priest declared an auspicious day to feed him, according to the prevailing planetary positions with reference to those in the baby's horoscope. Preparations began, clothes were distributed to the poor, sweets were distributed among each and every person in the kingdom; there were festivities everywhere. Somewhere deep in my heart, I was hoping and praying that Siddharth might pay us a visit—shouldn't he be a tiny bit curious about his son, I wondered.

I didn't wonder just once, but kept on wondering, and as the event drew nearer, the thought started consuming me. I believed if I thought hard enough, it would manifest. Wasn't it what grandma taught me? If you wish for something with your heart and soul, God hears you and delivers.

One evening, my ever-perceptive mother caught me folding and unfolding the festive little silk dresses that the royal seamstress had stitched for Rahul's feeding ceremony. I was quite lost and was brought back to the present by my mother's comment.

She said, 'There is suffering in everyone's life, it's a common phenomenon. But when extreme suffering knocks on our door, that is the moment when the ordinary path obtains extraordinary power to sustain our life and lead us towards freedom.'

Though my mother was successful in catching my

attention, I couldn't quite understand what she was trying to convey.

'All great inventions came about when the scientists were pushed to a corner from where there were no conventional ways of escape, so they had to invent their way out. Adversity is like a strong wind. It tears away from us all but the things that cannot be torn, so that we see ourselves as we really are. And what we really are, our core, is our strength, our resource to rebuild ourselves,' she continued patiently.

Mother said that I was living in a world of illusions and that my memories were of the husband I was in love with and wanted by my side. I was forgetting that Siddharth had changed, evolved over time. When he left, he was not what he was thirteen years ago.

This was the truth I was avoiding.

My mother left soon after the feeding ceremony, in which both the doting grandmothers of baby Rahul fed him with honey-sweetened rice pudding. It was his first step into the world of cereals. Since he had started teething too, Rahul loved every morsel of food that he was being fed that day, and everyday thereafter.

In my mother's absence I started ruminating on her last words of advice to me. I would lay awake at nights, wondering what could be my core strength. The answer didn't come then, but it came later, much later.

Six months after, my mother passed away peacefully under her favourite palash tree in the back garden, at dusk, communing with nature. Rahul was a one-year-old toddler then.

One day, on a whim, I decided to visit my father with Rahul. It was good that I did, because it was the only time my son could play with mud and be really close to nature, unhampered by the royal maids or servants fussing all around him.

My father had become quite lean and looked fragile. His calm, perceptive eyes that I remembered so fondly, were now tinged with sadness. Meeting his grandson brought back some life into him, and it made all three of us so happy. I decided to visit my father once a week.

These visits gave me the opportunity to visit the little shrine I had made as a child at the base of my mother's palash tree. I found that it lay undisturbed. Maybe my mother had looked after it; I would never know. The colourful pebbles seemed more deeply embedded in the soil and were now surrounded by a beautiful creeper with small succulent leaves and tiny yellow flowers. I didn't know the name of the plant, but it certainly added life to my little shrine.

My vegetable patch had grown bigger, as was expected, and qualified to be addressed as a garden now. As a child, I loved growing vegetables because the results were seen quicker than with fruits. Seeing light-green aubergines hiding among the leaves one day and then seeing them turn dark purple after a few days, used to fascinate me. Likewise for chilli plants—I loved seeing the chillies turn bright red from bright green. Apart from these, I grew onions and cauliflowers too, as well as coriander and mint.

As mentioned earlier, my father was a wealthy landlord who leased out lands mostly to farmers. The returns came in as money as well as produce. The land in our area was very fertile and gave good crops of wheat, rice, maize and many varieties of lentils. There were sugarcane plantations as well as mango and lychee orchards on our land. All that was my father's domain. My mother grew vegetables behind the kitchen of our house, while Grandma added herbs to it.

So, whatever vegetables we ate for our meals came from that kitchen garden. Basically, whatever we ate came from our own lands.

Reviving those memories was so cathartic that I decided to take a few saplings and some seeds back with me to the palace. I planned to create a small replica of our kitchen garden behind my rooms. It would become my personal garden, just like the peacock garden of my father-in-law. Feeling happy with my own idea, I decided to share it with my father and went looking for him. He was busy playing with Rahul, both equally delighted in each other's company. I didn't want to disturb them.

Seeing grandfather and grandson bonding over plants, pebbles and driftwood made me slip into an unconscious conversation with Siddharth, where I told him that had he spent his childhood like his son, maybe he would never have felt the need to leave…

Somehow, all my mental conversations with my husband would reach the point of his departure, and I would be shaken abruptly back to the present. Siddharth had left, but not from my mind, as yet.

It was not that I didn't try to get over my loss, but somehow, there were far too many things in my life to remind me of that dark night of betrayal. The only change that had happened in the past one year was that my anger had turned into sadness.

Slowly but surely, I was able to get over the waves of 'what if'. They were now limited to brief, very brief moments, practically a flashing thought, just like the one mentioned earlier. There was a time when every new action of Rahul would make me think that his father was missing seeing his son grow. And that very thought would propel me into a whirlpool of sadness. Not anymore.

I stopped diluting my happiness, my moments of wonder and awe on seeing my son grow day by day into a bright young boy.

According to my mother-in-law Queen Pajapati, Rahul was growing physically at a faster pace than his father. She gave the credit for that to his spending time with my father. Playing in and with nature had made little Rahul more dextrous with his limbs and alert with his senses.

One evening, as I sat with my father on the porch, sipping a warm herbal drink, we got to talking about my childhood. Watching Rahul trying to build a house with clay, sticks, stones and leaves reminded us of how I loved playing with clay, and how my mother had a tough time washing it off from my long hair. We had a great laugh visualizing all that. Later on though, I had given up messing about with clay and had shifted my attention to woodcraft.

Whenever we visited my father, I found that he would be talking a lot about my mother, reminiscing all the time. He must really be missing her so much, I thought. But he seemed at peace. So I asked, 'Father, how are you handling Mother's death? How are you coping with the loss?'

'I am not handling her death. I don't feel the loss. I am remembering her life, our life together. She's all around me, all the time. Each and every thing, every moment of the day, reminds me of her. And they are such wonderful memories,' he said with a smile.

Was it so simple? I wondered.

Exactly one year after my mother's death, my father passed away peacefully, sitting on the porch and overlooking the back garden...probably looking at my mother's favourite tree.

As I cried, I also felt that my parents must be reunited up in heaven. And this thought was somewhat comforting. It also made me realize how we draw our emotions from our thoughts. This was a breakthrough of sorts.

Since we drew all our emotions from our thoughts, it stood to reason that we should think good thoughts.

I looked at Rahul. My son was a two-year-old boy now. I had wasted two precious years wallowing in sad thoughts. 'Enough!' I said to myself. And just like that, literally in the snap of a finger, I felt lighter, better.

I learnt so much from my parents' lives, and more from their deaths. We learn all the time, from everyone, from every experience, don't we? Rahul must be learning from me. I had to be a good role model, but that too I learnt from my son. Let us see how.

6

ACCEPTANCE

The leaves had fallen, and along with the thirsty branches of the trees, I too awaited the cries of falcons and crows fleeing, as that would herald gusty storms followed by monsoon rains. Now that I had planted a vegetable patch, I looked forward to the natural watering of my saplings.

It was a normal day.

Rahul had gone to play with his friends as usual. Due to the faster pace of his cognitive development, he could comfortably play with children older than him. Siddharth had been a quick learner, according to my mother-in-law, but he was not as outgoing as his son. While Rahul loved being with people, Siddharth loved his own company the best.

There were a couple of children of the palace staff who were good company for my son. It was a kind of done thing in the palace, as all of Siddharth's friends were also like that. For instance, the royal priest's son and the chief minister's son were friends of my husband. Likewise, their sons were friends of my son.

That evening, Rahul returned to our chambers looking

despondent. He didn't take much interest in eating either; he just came and snuggled with me in my bed.

'Where is my Baba? My friends say he has gone away. When will he return? Why has he gone? All of them have Babas. I don't!' Rahul never seemed to ask one question. When he asked anything, it was always a bunch of questions, one toppling over the other.

'Of course you have a Baba, like everyone else, my dear!' I hugged my fast-growing baby. How time flew, and how my baby whose eyes looked only for me were now suddenly looking for his father. In any case, how long can these things remain hidden anyway.

'I made a cat and a monkey with clay, just as Nana taught me. But I don't know how to make a horse. Jaidev knows how to make a horse. His Baba taught him. Nana is also gone. Who will teach me?'

Nana, my father, had taught quite a few things to Rahul in the last few months that we were visiting him. I realized I had to take over that role.

'I will. I know how to make all the animals of the world with clay. I know how to make houses too, and also men, women and children.' Oh, it was such a pleasure to see that smile lighting up my son's face, as his little brain planned his clay-building agenda for the forthcoming days.

'You know, dear, that people become old and sick like your Nana. You have also seen how everyone gets worried when someone they love falls sick. Your Baba saw all this and decided to help people by finding a cure for it. He wanted everyone to be happy. So, one day, he decided to look for this cure and off he went!'

It was not that Rahul didn't know about his father's going away; he was just too young to understand the finality of it.

'Dada said he looks after everyone. Baba didn't have to go. He could have told Dada. Then Dada would have helped. That is his job, isn't it?' Rahul addressed my father-in-law as Dada.

'Yes, it is Dada's job to help people. But you see, we have a huge kingdom, with so many people and their many problems. Poor Dada is so busy all the time. Baba decided to help his father by taking care of some of his work. Remember when Nana was teaching you to make clay animals, he told you to help him by rolling the clay into tails for those animals? It is something like that. You and your Nana made animals together. In the same way, Baba and Dada are helping the people of our kingdom together, to keep them happy.'

'Okay,' sighed Rahul, and continued almost immediately, 'but when will Baba return?'

That was a tough one to answer.

'Baba will return when he has found what he has gone looking for.'

Fortunately, this extremely unsatisfactory answer satisfied the two-year-old. He snuggled further into my bed and slept peacefully. And for the next five years, there were no questions from him about his father.

How innocent is a child's mind and how trusting, I thought as I stroked my son's thatch of silky black hair.

I remembered my father's words: 'It is difficult to accept our loss. That done, we need to acknowledge our pain, as facing it is the only way to go through it. The toughest part is to adjust to our loved one's absence. Gradually, over time, we let go of sadness and learn to live with the happy memories and move on in life.'

I made a few decisions. The most important amongst them was that I would teach my son what my father taught me: he would not live a mollycoddled life as his father did. Rahul would live in the real world.

I had already planted a vegetable garden with the help of Narayani, Rohini's younger sister. I decided to introduce Rahul to plants, the way my grandmother did, through stories first, followed later on by actual handling.

I also planned to take Rahul for outings and show him the countryside. He lived the life of a prince, as was expected. But I wanted to enrich my son further by introducing him to the kind of life I had led. Maybe, somewhere deep in my heart, I felt that my son should not feel the need to look for some missing part of his life, as his father did. Little did I know then that one's search is one's own, and nobody can have a say in it or influence it in any way.

Months flew by, then a year; the seasons rolled on. The trees in the vast palace grounds blossomed, then shed their leaves, only to come alive again in the seasonal cycles. In the thirteen years that Siddharth and I spent together, I had seen but ignored the trees. But now, I saw them in all their glory. It was as though we lived in a bubble, which Siddharth burst as he left. I had been reluctant to step out of it in the vain hope that my husband would return. But now that I had stepped out of it, the friendly colourful world of nature opened up for me. The vast palace grounds seemed to be a giant canvas showcasing nature's beauty.

Dotting the grounds, the kadamb trees bloomed with exotic yellow blossoms tinged with pink, huddled together in bunches. Bordering the royal gardens were the tall champak trees whose strongly fragrant yellow-orange flowers were subsequently used by Narayani to make my jewellery.

Then there were clusters of prickly pangar trees, whose shining red blossoms in full bloom became like open aviaries, attracting a host of birds such as mynahs, crows, babblers and parakeets, as well as swarms of bees and wasps. I had heard much about ashoka trees from my grandmother. Here, we had a grove of these sacred trees covered with lush balls of blossoms turning from orange to red.

Ah, the rows and rows of flaming red palash, my mother's favourite! Bordering the avenues that criss-crossed the palace grounds, these trees confronted me every day, as though designed to remind me of her unfading presence in my life.

Closer to the three royal seasonal palaces, I was fascinated by the regal elegance of the mahaasona trees covered in bunches of pale purple flowers standing arrogantly, as opposed to the normally drooping ones of other trees. In contrast were the magnificent yellow cascading blooms of the amaltas trees that shed at the slightest breeze, spreading cheer wherever they fell, and they did fall a lot.

I could go on and on.

While I was appreciating the artistry of nature, my precocious son was conquering the hearts of everyone in and around the palace. Every other day, there would be some gifts or the other for the youngest royal—ranging from intricately carved little furniture to exquisitely embroidered fine silk clothes, to beautifully crafted colourful toys, to all kinds of sweets. My father-in-law had started lining up tutors to teach various subjects to Rahul. It seemed as though King Shuddhodhan had reversed time; he started looking and behaving like his younger self of twenty years ago.

With Rahul's attention being diverted by so many people, I had more time for myself now. I would sit with my mother-in-law as she held her little court, a place where any woman could come and air her grievances or share her pain.

Queen Pajapati was not offering anything to these women except a listening ear and a compassionate heart. In her court, she was not queen, nor were those women her subjects; they were all at one level, that of women. I saw that each one of those women had suffered and somehow, the others could relate to that suffering. Some had advice to give, some just solace, but all listened to and shared the pain.

Every time after attending these meetings, I would go and sit by the lotus pond and contemplate the stories of these women. How selfish I had been to believe that my suffering was the greatest. It was a humbling realization.

Three years ago, my mother had said the same thing to me and I had paid no heed. I guess things happen when they have to happen. Perhaps I was not ready then. Perhaps I was ready now.

Then, one day, I opened my heart in front of the women and was overwhelmed by the collective show of compassion and love from them. I had not realized how much I had bottled up inside myself till then. I broke down as I had never done before, even with my own mother. The women hugged me and cried with me. The entire experience was unexpectedly quite cathartic.

As I sat later that evening dining with my mother-in-law, she remarked, 'Sometimes we need the light of others to see the way. Sometimes we need to be a light for others. This is common knowledge. But the most interesting thing I have seen is that the light shines more brightly when two or more of them are together.'

It was such a simple yet profound observation.

As more months rolled by, I realized that when I was suffering in isolation, within my own self, I was actually spreading suffering all around. People who loved and cared for me suffered seeing me suffer. But when I opened up and shared my suffering with others, by talking and listening to them in a kind of shared communion, it brought me immense peace. In fact, being with suffering seemed to bring peace to all. I was gradually understanding the real meaning of acceptance.

During my long walks in the palace gardens, I had made it a habit to rest under Siddharth's favourite rose-apple tree. One such day, I realized that I could actually see my thoughts come and go through my head in a detached manner. I had become an observer of my own thoughts. It was fascinating! Being silently watchful, neither for nor against.

I discovered another interesting phenomenon—at the

height of emotion, if I became conscious, I was suddenly engulfed in calmness. It was as though that emotion fell away from me on its own, effortlessly.

I was still conversing with Siddharth in my mind those days, but differently than before, so I promptly shared my new discovery with him. I had taken this business of sharing very seriously, as the very fact, the very act of sharing, whether physical or mental, was extremely gratifying and lightening… to not be carrying the burden of thoughts.

In the past one year, I had developed a detached attachment of sorts with my husband too. Instead of a physical presence, he had become a mental presence in my life. No, I was not going mad. In fact, I had never felt saner than I did then.

My awareness of my own thoughts also trickled down to the awareness of my entire physical, material body. It did not happen in one day. Over the course of time, I began to give away my fine clothes and jewels to women who attended Queen Pajapati's court. They needed those things more than me. I had started wearing mostly white or light-coloured handwoven cottons or muslins and had cut my hair short to a manageable length.

By the end of that year, I had also dismissed my numerous maids, except Rohini, who was more like a companion to me. Her sister Narayani continued to help me in my gardening activities. She was blessed with green fingers, and I learnt much from her.

I would wake up early, before sunrise, and come out of my room, to return to it only after sunset. Since my material desires had gone, my meals also became smaller and simpler. People assumed that I was trying to follow my husband's footsteps by adopting austerities. It was not so. I was not following any person, I was following my heart.

When I gained control over my mind, my desires lost their power to tempt me. I did not feel the need for so much of the material wealth that surrounded me. Hence, I started giving away what was mine, to those whom I felt needed it more.

Likewise, my body did not feel the need to consume rich foods. It felt happier and healthier partaking in the simple bounties of nature, like the fresh fruits of the season and vegetables from my little garden, nuts, honey and cow's milk. I did not deliberately start eating less, I just lost my appetite, and ate what my body needed to function optimally.

Of course I knew that Siddharth was living a frugal existence somewhere in the forests, near the kingdom of Magadh—that was the path he had chosen for himself. I was not emulating him. I was making my own path, guided by nature. Everything was happening organically with me, with no effort whatsoever from my side.

King Shuddhodhan had deputed his men to gain information about Siddharth. Earlier he had sent his chief minister to try and convince the prince to return to look after the kingdom, but in vain. The minister came back convinced that Siddharth was on the path to find happiness for the entire world and should not be disturbed.

'Tell my father not to worry about the throne of Kapilvastu. The throne will find a king for itself,' was Siddharth's message for King Shuddhodhan.

Thereafter, the king sent men only to keep track of his son, like any protective father. We were aware that Siddharth was studying scriptures under the religious teachers Alara Kalama and Udraka Ramaputra. They wanted him to stay on with them and teach other seekers, but Siddharth's search was not over as yet. He wanted to experiment on himself with whatever knowledge he had acquired.

By this time, people had begun to revere him as a learned monk.

We came to know that once Siddharth went to beg in Rajgriha, the capital city of the kingdom of Magadh. King Bimbisar happened to see him and was deeply impressed by Siddharth's noble bearing, which was unlike that of any monk he had come across. The following day, Bimbisar paid a visit to Siddharth's dwelling to invite him. The king of Magadh wanted Siddharth to live with him as his advisor, offering half the kingdom in return. Refusing politely, Siddharth explained his quest to the king, and promised to return once he found the answers.

Back home, at the palace, the healing power of Queen Pajapati's court was spreading beyond the walls and boundaries of the kingdom. Now women came to share not only their sorrows but also their happiness.

One day, a young widow called Kisa attended Pajapati's court. She was the widow of a rich landowner. Becoming a widow in those times was considered to be a curse. Somehow, the woman was always blamed for her husband's death and was abandoned by the husband's family, along with her children, if any. Afraid of the social censure, the parents of the woman would also disown her.

In Kisa's case, when she was abandoned by her in-laws, she had a baby son who was quite sickly. She tried to look after her baby by begging, but as fate would have it, the baby died. Kisa could not or would not accept that her baby was dead and continued carrying its body all over the village, crying out for help.

By chance, a monk was passing through that village. The villagers told Kisa to meet him and seek his help. Kisa went crying to the monk, showing him the dead baby, and begging him to bring it to life. The monk told her that he would certainly do so if she could get him a handful of mustard seeds from any family where no one had died.

Poor Kisa went to every house in the village, but could not find any family where no one had died. She realized the harsh truth that death and the suffering associated with it were unavoidable. She buried her son and came to share her story at Queen Pajapati's court.

My mother-in-law was so overwhelmed listening to the story that she invited Kisa to stay on in the palace. The thought that the monk in the story could have been Siddharth might have also played a role in her taking that decision.

My days were divided into time spent with my mother-in-law and her court of ladies, time spent with Rahul, and time spent with my own self, which took up the maximum number of hours. I loved my walks within the palace grounds and sometimes into the fields beyond.

Rahul was being increasingly engaged by his tutors, under his grandfather's watchful eyes. King Shuddhodhan was convinced that his grandson was two, or maybe more, years ahead of his peers. Fortunately for him, Rahul's tutors agreed with the king's hypothesis.

So while the king focused on his agenda of grooming his grandson to become the next ruler of the Shakya kingdom, the queen was gently empowering the women of the kingdom. The king was imposing a multitude of skills on young Rahul. The queen was exposing the inner strengths of the women.

One day, at Queen Pajapati's court, a woman by the name of Jayanti seemed rather distracted. Normally, the women came not only to discuss their own joys and sorrows, but also to resolve their problems, and sometimes to only listen to other women. Listening to others, as I had also experienced, was like a balm to the soul. Jayanti was one such listener. But that day, she was unable to pay attention to anyone.

Kisa, who had by now firmly attached herself like a shadow to Queen Pajapati, queried Jayanti on her distracted state.

'My daughter's marriage has been fixed. Now my husband says we should thank the Mother Goddess with goat's blood. And, after the sacrifice, we should hold a feast for our community. According to him, doing this will ensure our daughter's happiness after marriage. But I wonder what happens in those communities that do not follow this tradition. Are those women unhappy in their marriages?'

Jayanti's question opened up a topic that was hitherto considered sacrosanct. How can killing an animal be considered good for any reason whatsoever! I was reminded of Siddharth's childhood incident of saving an injured swan and glanced at my mother-in-law. She had the same opinion as she had then—when it comes to killing or saving a life, the latter is more empowering.

As women, we all knew what went into giving birth to another life. So, being inherent nurturers, it would be unimaginable for us to snuff out a life.

That day, all the women at Queen Pajapati's court unanimously agreed to boycott animal sacrifice. Together, we empowered each other. The deep bonds that we had organically created amongst ourselves had transformative power beyond our imagination. The beauty of all this being that it was a result of sharing as equals without being judgemental.

The more time I spent with these women, and there were different ones every day, the more I saw how participating in a meaningful relationship with everyone, all living things, all creation, is the centre of our life, human life.

Meanwhile, Rahul turned six. This was followed by the news that Siddharth had become the Buddha, under a peepal tree, on the banks of the river Niranjana in Uruvela, a small village in Magadh.

This was great news as Siddharth had achieved what he had set out for, but it also sealed the fact that now he would never return home. In fact, as the Buddha, Siddharth would go even further from us, from his immediate family. The world was his family now; he belonged to everyone. He belonged to no one.

King Shuddhodhan declared that Rahul's training to become a king should begin as soon as possible. This sudden knee-jerk decision was his way of showing that he still retained control, if not on his son, then at least on his grandson. Queen Pajapati managed to get her husband to defer this decision by one year, and we all heaved a sigh of relief. Precocious he might be intellectually, but Rahul had the body of a six-year-old. He was certainly not ready, physically, to be trained as a warrior.

One evening, I sat near the lotus pond as usual, but this time I observed. The lotus roots were buried in mud. Some stems had reached the surface of the water, but not risen above, while some had barely emerged to reveal curled-up leaves that were about to open. There were unopened lotus buds, and those with petals just beginning to peek out, and of course many lotus flowers in full bloom. Then there were seed pods from which all the petals had fallen. There were three colours of lotuses: white, pink and blue.

Weren't we like these lotuses? Everyone different in their looks and ages, and in different stages of mental and physical development, yet living together harmoniously in the same pond-like world.

Channa came by. I had once told him to keep an eye on and look after Siddharth, and he had taken it very seriously. Channa made it his life's mission to keep track of his Master, as he called him, and report back to me. King Shuddhodhan had also deputed his men to keep him updated on his son's whereabouts, but I felt more comfortable with my own deputy.

'I need to share something with you, My Lady.' He seemed a little hesitant.

I gestured to him to sit, but he preferred to stand, as always.

'I met Master Anand yesterday. He is one of the very few close to Master Buddha who are fortunate to learn from him. Out of the many things he has learnt, Master Anand taught me the most important one. It is watching my breath, which I want to share with you. According to him, we should continue sharing what we keep learning.'

'Yes Channa, that is the right thing to do. Not only what we learn, but also our sorrows and joys should be shared. Her Majesty Queen Pajapati holds a court every day, a court of shared communion. Would you like to share your learning there? With all of us?'

'If you don't mind, My Lady, I would like to share with you and you may share further.'

I did not pressure him, as I knew how shy Channa was.

'It is very simple. Master Anand taught me to sit silently with eyes closed and pay attention to my breathing. After a moment or two, we are able to notice our breath coming in and going out. But then our attention drifts because of some turmoil in our mind. We need to face that turmoil, become familiar with it, so familiar that it stops bothering us and drops away. And our attention is back on our breath. In this way, all our troubling thoughts leave us one by one, and we are at peace.'

Channa looked visibly relieved and tranquil after sharing this gem.

'Thank you Channa. I will surely share this with the other ladies at the queen's court.'

I didn't have the heart to tell him that I had discovered this mindfulness technique a while back. What delighted me was that Siddharth and I seemed to be walking on the same path, though I was in the palace and he was outside it. Such was the depth of our bond.

'What else did you learn?'

Channa had to be prodded all the time. It was as though he had lost all words. Kanthak, Siddharth's horse, had collapsed on his way back that fateful night, and passed away. Since Channa's life revolved around Siddharth and his mount Kanthak, the shock of losing both created a huge vacuum in him, where his words had also probably drowned.

'Master Buddha says that we should avoid the two extremes of sensual pleasures and practising extreme austerities. They lead us to self-destruction. Instead, we should follow the middle path of moderation. Hearing this, Yash, son of one of the richest merchants of Benares, left everything and has become Master Buddha's follower, along with his friends.

'Yash was unhappy with his rich, purposeless life. They had so much money that all he did was spend it on friends and the other pleasures of life. One day, he was walking in the deer park in Isipatana, near Benares, mumbling and grumbling to himself about how everything around him had started revolting him. Fortunately, Master Buddha, who was present in the park, heard him. He called him and explained that nothing was revolting. It was because he was overindulging himself that he now felt disgusted.'

Anyway, to cut the long story short, Channa said that Yash was so impressed by Siddharth's explanation that he never went back home, and became a monk. Seeing him, a number of his friends also left their homes and joined the brotherhood of sorts that Siddharth seemed to have created in Isipatana.

I felt sad for the families of those youths.

Moderation as a key to happiness was common sense that ultimately everyone realized at some time or the other in their lives, I thought to myself in amusement. Maybe not those living in affluence, but the ones who lead normal lives manage to reach this conclusion in their lifetimes.

'You are right about moderation, Channa. It is like eating food. You feel sick if you overeat. At the same time, if you starve yourself, then also you feel sick. In the extreme of both cases, you can actually die. The best then would be to eat what your body needs, isn't it!'

Channa agreed with me with a smile. It was his first smile in six years. He probably saw Siddharth's words echoing in me and felt comforted. So much so that he seemed to be wanting to talk more. A man with very little words had suddenly transformed into one with a never-ending flow of sentences. This was a miracle indeed!

After becoming the Buddha, Siddharth went to Benares to look for his old friends who had meditated with him in the past. Once they understood what the Buddha's path was, they became his followers. Then Yash joined them, and so on. Siddharth had promised to meet King Bimbisar once he found his answers, so he decided to go to Rajgriha next. On the way, he stopped at Niranjana River again to spend some time at the spot where he had awakened.

Across the river, a large group of mendicants had made their way to the hermitage by now. Siddharth went to meet them. Their leader was Kassapa. These mendicants worshipped fire as god and reared animals for sacrifice. They never went to the village for food; the villagers themselves came with their daily offerings. Kassapa was a Vedic scholar.

Siddharth had long discussions about the Vedas, Upanishads and other scriptures with Kassapa, for many days. To Kassapa's argument of fire being the ultimate purifier, Siddharth asked about those who bathed in river Ganga to be purified. There were arguments and counter-arguments, till Siddharth put forward his theories of inter-dependence and impermanence, and how understanding these fundamental truths could protect us from suffering, not by praying to fire.

This was a turning point in Kassapa's life. He, his brothers, and hundreds of his followers became monks and joined the Buddha's sangha, as the brotherhood was now called.

I was awestruck by this story. Siddharth the Buddha must have struck a deep chord in people for them to leave their own well-trodden path to follow his unique one.

Channa left, and I was back with my lotuses. I observed them yet again...inter-dependence.

It was true that the lotus blooms I was appreciating did not appear just like that. Like all plants, there has to be a seed at the beginning of their journey of life. The seed stays in the soil or mud for a while to absorb water, so that the tiny plant embryo in it wakes up and comes out. After which, with the help of sunshine, water and food from its habitat, the plant sapling grows and develops its stem, leaves, flowers, fruits and its own seeds. All the elements of heat, light, air, water, food, collectively help it grow from a seed to a flower or a fruit. If any of these elements is missing, the flower or fruit will not exist. This is the power of inter-dependence.

Our existence is because of others. One does not exist without the other.

Siddharth was already sceptical about Vedic chanting, as he had told his mother during the ploughing festival, at the tender age of nine years. He could see even then that the chanting was not helping the tiny helpless creatures survive, so his lengthy discussions with Kassapa were not unusual.

Channa's references to the fire-god and sacrifice reminded me of Jayanti's case of animal sacrifice. In my opinion, nothing should be converted to a ritual. We had already started a movement against animal sacrifice amongst the women, thanks to Jayanti. Hopefully, from what I understood, Siddharth would now be able to convince people against rituals like fire sacrifice, which involved praying and pouring of cereals, pulses, clarified butter, etc., into fire to appease the gods.

As far as sacrifices go, come to think of it, Siddharth sacrificed his family for the sake of finding the right path for people. Maybe not a traditional ritualistic sacrifice, yet a sacrifice it was, for him as well as for us. I sincerely hoped it was worth it.

Today, as I awaited my husband, who was now becoming famous as the Buddha, I wondered what new I would discover in him, and through him, in myself.

So far, we seemed to be walking on parallel paths.

7

HOMECOMING

There was a gentle knock at the door. I took a deep breath and turned my head towards the door that I once hated so much.

'Blessings Yasho,' Siddharth said in a soft melodious voice, or maybe it was my imagination that made his words sound like music to my ears.

There was a majesty about him now, not the kingly majesty but a holy one. Tall and graceful, with his shoulders pulled back like a well-trained archer, and eyes that seemed like pools of eternity, capable of drowning the entire world. Siddharth looked more beautiful than ever today.

I looked at him, searching to find who he was that stood there before me. Images of the past twenty years of the restless, tormented, sensual lover and husband clashed with this new calm person with a steady gaze, the Awakened One, the Buddha. It was like standing in a dense forest of very tall trees with the sun shining above but the wind blowing, and the trees swaying to create a psychedelic atmosphere of a play of light and shade.

It was an unearthly, timeless moment.

As we looked at each other after a separation of seven years, Siddharth's eyes welled up, and a teardrop escaped from the corner of his left eye. That was the only emotion I saw, and that too was not really an emotion so much as the result of an emotion. It revealed his understanding of the depth of my emotions. Other than that, his eyes, his face, his entire demeanour exuded unwavering serenity and compassion. My Siddharth, who was such a gentle human, had become more ardently so—his immensity seemed uncontainable now.

In that shared moment of ours, I could see him reading me as I read him. That was our special bond, a bond of shared lifetimes. We could read each other like open books…and suddenly it struck me that maybe that's why he didn't want me to see him leaving—he couldn't have left then.

Today, as I saw him, I also saw us being seen by each other. It was like being an observer and the observed at the same time. A liberating feeling indeed!

'What brought you back?' I asked before I could stop myself. And well, my forthrightness had not diminished over the years, as a slight smile on Siddharth's face indicated.

'I had promised you through Channa that I would come after I had found my answers. I had to come, at least once. King Shuddhodhan also doesn't have much time left.'

I was a bit thrown off by that statement, as my father-in-law seemed in perfect health to me.

'I came to make amends to you, and through you, to the others. I am profoundly sorry for the pain I caused you, Yasho…'

My astonishment on hearing this overlapped with an immense wave of relief and gratitude.

'It was very hard for me to leave you and our son that night, because I was too attached at that time…to you, and our baby. And like all attachments, it was selfish. I had to let go of that kind of love, if I was ever going to find the answers I was looking for. I wanted to learn the kind of love that went beyond individuals, the kind that was beyond suffering.'

'You wanted the answer to suffering, but caused suffering to all of us in order to find it,' I couldn't resist adding.

He smiled his old indulgent smile and continued, 'After our son was born, I came to see the two of you in your room. You seemed very tired, and I didn't want to disturb you. I wanted to hold our son in my arms, but knew it would wake you. I also knew that I would lose the courage I needed to leave, if you woke up and we saw each other. At that point, a word flashed across my mind—Rahul—meaning obstacle…'

'Are you saying that you thought of his name even before the royal priest drew up his horoscope?' I was absolutely astounded.

'Yes, I did. His birth created an obstacle. At that time, both of you were obstacles. Had I lingered, I would never have achieved what I knew needed to be achieved, and so I left. I had to sever the bonds that caused suffering—to me—if answers were ever to be found.'

'Yes, I have also realized it since then…bonds do cause suffering.'

'I have heard about the good work you are doing, Yasho. You are helping people heal themselves. Unknown to you, in doing all this, you are actually walking beside me, as you have always done.'

Thus validating my life in a single stroke, Siddharth went over to sit on the wooden bench near the window.

'I must share my discoveries with you, for haven't I always done that?'

This innocent remark dissolved my leftover defences completely and I sat on the bed, ready with a listening ear, just the way I used to when we were together… whenever…wherever we were together.

'Birth alone is the cause of old age, sickness and death. This is a simple enough observation. Whoever is born has to go through sickness, old age, and finally death. There is absolutely no escaping that. Everyone knows this. But, as you know, it bothered me.'

Siddharth took a deep breath and continued.

'I went to look for a teacher, one who might know the way to reach the answers. On asking around, I was directed to Master Alara Kalama, who had a hermitage near Vaishali, the capital of the Licchavi kingdom. I joined him, and that's where I was shown how to beg, how to receive the food offerings, and how to thank those who made the offerings. I also learnt how to rid myself of thoughts of the past and future. Soon, I could meditate and reach the state where my mind became one with infinity; it seemed limitless…' he paused briefly.

'It was a glorious feeling, Yasho. Yet, my mind was still not liberated from my deepest anxieties and sorrows.

During my meditations, I could see that my mind was present in every phenomenon in the universe, and also that the entire universe was created by my own mind. All this profound understanding did not help resolve the fundamental problem of birth and death, suffering and anxiety. Master Kalama had nothing more to teach and asked me join him in teaching other monks. I declined the offer politely and left.'

'What you experienced is the essence of our scriptures, isn't it,' I commented softly.

'Yes.' He moved on, 'The next teacher I met was Master Udraka Ramaputra near Rajgriha. He taught me how to transcend perception, entering a state of unconsciousness. But that too was not the key to liberation from life and death. Master Ramaputra asked me to join him in teaching other monks. I had to refuse him too. When I left, five more disciples left with me.

'I wondered why we needed to follow the traditions laid out in the scriptures, because that was what all the masters learnt and taught from. Why should our goal always be to find the means to escape the world of feeling and thought, the world of sensation and perception?'

'Didn't you do just that?! That is our conditioning, the foundation on which our society, everyone, everything exists.'

I had to put in my two bits, because what Siddharth was saying today was what he himself did seven years ago... escape the world of feeling. As far as the scriptures were concerned, he had always questioned their usefulness to the common man.

'The fundamental issue of liberation from suffering still burnt within me,' Siddharth continued, ignoring my interruption.

'I decided to be my own teacher. From there, I went to the Dangsiri Mountain near Uruvela and decided to meditate in one of the caves, and review whatever I had learnt thus far. It had been five years since I left, and I wanted to consolidate all the knowledge gleaned over that period and check for any gaps. I had done everything, experienced everything, except self-mortification. I remembered that once I had met an emaciated ascetic sitting, possibly meditating, on a rock in harsh sunlight. The rock was burning hot and the man was sweating. I was amazed at the sight and curious too, so waited patiently for him to open his eyes. Finally, when he did so, I asked him the reason for whatever he was doing. He said that our bodies are full of desires and, hence, unfit for enlightenment, just like damp wood is unfit for being lit. Self-mortification, according to him, helped him get rid of his desires, and expedite his journey to liberation.

'So, taking that as a path to follow, I sat in a cave meditating, fighting my fears of darkness, of wild animals, snakes and the like. A couple of months later, the five monks of Master Ramaputra found me and joined me in this journey. We decided that one of us would go into town to beg for food and divide that amongst the six of us. That was all that we ate in a day. Days and months passed by, and we started looking like that emaciated ascetic. Ultimately, none of us had the strength to go to the town to beg. We decided to leave the caves and move closer to

Niranjana River, where at least we didn't have to make much effort in getting water. There we ate whatever fruits or berries we found on the ground. Many days, I wouldn't even do that much, as my aim was self-mortification after all. We meditated wherever we felt like, the pebbled riverbank or the nearby cremation ground, anywhere at all.'

I was horrified trying to picture my handsome husband as an emaciated ascetic with long beard and even longer hair.

'One evening, as I sat meditating, a cool breeze began to flow. After sitting the entire day under the blazing sun, the breeze felt refreshing and my mind relaxed, as it had not done in the past many, many months. It came as a flash to me that body and mind were one single reality that could not be separated. I was torturing my body, so how could my mind be at peace! I also recalled my first meditation under the rose-apple tree—how when my mind was at ease, I could observe better. I reached the conclusion that I would resume begging to nourish my physical body and meditate to nourish my mind.

'I bathed in the Niranjana, but fainted on the riverbank. When I opened my eyes next, I saw this young girl trying to feed me rice porridge. She was Sujata. I felt strength returning to my body and gave up the very thought of self-mortification right away.'

A gentle smile played on Siddharth's face while reminiscing those times.

'I decided to return to myself and be present in the world of phenomena. There was a beautiful giant peepal tree near the riverbank that became my refuge. There was enough kusha grass for me to sleep on under the tree. Sujata and her friends from the village started bringing food for me. Everything happened after that.'

'Are you saying that what didn't happen in five years happened in five months?'

'Maybe yes, may no. You see, Yasho, I believe it was a cumulative effect of my entire life, including those five years, till the point that propelled me to make the breakthrough I did in five months or maybe five weeks, and awaken to the reality of life.'

'I guess it's the same as my mother always said, that once we feel cornered we find a way out. And what did those five monks have to say about this development?'

'It was more like when you continue adding salt to water, there comes a point when that water can't take it anymore. At that point, if you add even one tiny grain of salt, it results in the entire salt, which was hitherto hidden in water, to suddenly crystallize out of it. As for the other monks, have patience, I am getting there.'

Amused by my impatience, my husband smiled.

The past seven years dissolved in seven moments, and it felt the same as it did when we chatted while walking miles across the green fields, or sitting under a shady tree. I had made many good friends in my life, but the kind of friendship I shared with my husband was undefinable and irreplaceable.

'My monk companions lost faith in me when they saw me abandoning the path of self-mortification, and left,' Siddharth responded to my query.

'Existence was, is, full of objects one can meditate upon. I did just that. In seeing all things in myself and myself in all things, I realized that this life, in all its stages, is an outward appearance of but one aspect of existence. And is not in itself a true reality. Existence is vast otherwise, and is ever flowing, ever changing, ever dynamic. It encompasses all living beings. But we believe in the existence of our separate selves. That, and our illusion of permanence, is the source of our suffering. This is ignorance. Removal of ignorance alleviates suffering. And the only way to remove ignorance is through wisdom.'

'But you reject the very scriptures that are the sources of all knowledge, all wisdom,' I tried to provoke, albeit unsuccessfully.

'Wisdom is different from knowledge, Yasho. The scriptures may give us knowledge, but that does not necessarily make us wise. Wisdom means knowing the nature of conditions as we are experiencing them, without getting caught up in reacting to them or getting attached to them. It means to be able to see that the conditions are constantly changing. I refer to this "knowing of the change" as "buddha", and tell people to take refuge in it, to submit to that wisdom of being aware, of being awake.'

It was gratifying to learn that Siddharth and I really did achieve similar milestones, though following different paths.

'The second refuge that I offer is that of "dhamma" or the ultimate truth, the ultimate reality,' continued Siddharth, the Buddha.

'Dhamma is not good or bad. It just is. It is the here and now, the present moment. Unbound by any time condition, it is timeless. Our mind is constantly taking us away from the present, into the future or the past. Dhamma wakes us up from that delusional state and brings us to the here and now.

'The third refuge is that of "sangha", which means a group, more or less of like-minded people who live virtuously. Being a part of such a group is a practical way of imbibing virtue in our day-to-day lives. Everyone has, or can have, good as well as bad thoughts and intentions, which guide our actions. In this ever-changing world, keeping a constant check on one's thoughts may not be very easy. Living in a sangha helps, as people help each other to help themselves. It teaches one to live mindfully in relation to other living beings of this world.'

Wasn't this exactly what I had learnt! I told Siddharth so: 'I seem to have inadvertently created or maybe stumbled upon the hidden path of shared communion. By sharing, I embraced the "we", and my "self" was released. I became aware of the oneness of life. I could simultaneously see, plainly and clearly, all that existed inside and outside of me. And I realized how we built our world of illusions and then ended up getting trapped in it.'

As I spoke these words, I was transported back to when Siddharth and I used to sit near the lotus pond and talk our hearts out.

'As you have seen yourself by now, Yasho, you and I have journeyed on similar paths, the difference being that I discovered buddha first and you discovered sangha.'

Listening to Siddharth was like recapping the last seven years of my life. It was as though he had picked up all the precious moments, the various breakthroughs I had had, and strung them together to give them a sort of coherence, making them meaningful…somewhat like collecting and stringing scattered pearls to make a necklace out of them.

Earlier, I would create meaning out of his rambling thoughts for him. Our roles had reversed, I mused.

'To see is to love, to love is to understand, to understand is to transcend the ignorance that binds. You are free, Yasho…as free as me. Now we must continue journeying on our paths and spread this wisdom.'

While speaking, Siddharth's eyes held mine and a bolt of lightning passed through my entire body, jolting me up to stand. He got up too. Our meeting was over.

'Today, as I stand before you, Siddharth, the Buddha, I can happily say that you did the right thing that night when you left us. For if you hadn't, I would not have discovered my own path. And for that, I shall remain eternally grateful to you.'

It was time to say goodbye, and Siddharth voiced the words that were echoing in my heart since the morning, the words I was, if not dreading, then most reluctant to hear.

'Rahul asked me for his inheritance when he came to meet me. And what we have here, what I carry with me is his inheritance, which I offered to him. He asked to accompany me.'

There it was, put so succinctly. I had no words to add. As the father left the room, his son entered.

'Mother, have you heard!' he rushed to hug me.

'Yes, dear son, I have. But I think you are too young yet. There are no boys in the sangha, I believe.'

'Yes, I know. And I shall be the first boy!' Rahul's excitement was palpable.

'Are you aware of the hardships you would have to face? You, who has lived a protected, almost cushioned life, will have to live in the forest and walk in all kinds of weather.'

I tried to show the ground reality to my son, the prince of Kapilvastu. His father had left at the ripe old age of twenty-nine, but Rahul was a mere seven-year-old child—even his milk teeth hadn't quite been replaced yet by permanent ones. Though I knew the futility of damming the flow of water, as we saw in my husband's case, I felt I had to try.

'Yes, and I will have to beg once a day for food, listen to my father's discourses, practise mindful breathing, and follow what the other monks do. Do not worry about me, Ma. I am after all my father's son, and shall be living with him.'

How simple he made it sound! He really was his father's son. Rahul had grown up, grown up real fast—I had to let go.

8

DEPARTURE

I hugged my son again—a longer, tighter hug—our final hug before we went down together where the monks were waiting for him. My Rahul was stepping out into the world today…and would cease to be mine henceforth.

As my little prince shed his royal garments and donned the ochre robes, my heart skipped a beat. A lump rose in my throat as I saw Rahul following his father with an ebony begging bowl in his hand, and a spring in his step. My eyes dimmed with tears that flowed unrestrained. I clenched and unclenched my fists and started breathing deeply to hang on to my self-control, which was precariously close to breaking down. I reminded myself repeatedly to not be selfish, to trust that my son would be looked after well by his father.

It was a tough call, but I did it.

Dusk fell as the dust of a thousand—plus a little one—retreating monks followed the Buddha out of the city.

I went up to my balcony, from where I could see the fading away of the ochre wave that had come like a tsunami to change the course of my life, yet again.

I sat on the marble bench, feeling empty, like a blank page, like a sandy beach that had been washed clean by the waves. My palms were hurting where my own nails had dug into and bruised them while clenching hard.

Hours passed. The sky lost its red hue of sunset and started darkening… My attention was caught by the bright evening star, shining steadfastly in the sky, as though telling me that the spark of life was not dead yet. Staring at the vast boundless sky as the rest of the stars started appearing slowly, I realized that love is equally boundless, and we have no business to bind it down to a few relationships.

Limited love has a tendency to grow claws with which we grip the person to whom we are bound. While we think of it as love, it has already turned to poison for the one whom we are gripping with them. When that person frees himself from their grip, that love of ours rebounds to us and poisons our heart against the very person we love. It's amazing how easily love can turn from being benign to malignant in a split second. I shuddered at the thought and shook it off.

Going back to my room, I asked Rohini to get me writing materials. I decided to put down my thoughts and reflections in a journal… That was the day I started writing this journal, vowing never to stop till my last breath.

The palace seemed so empty after Rahul's departure, but it was a different kind of emptiness this time. On Siddharth's leaving, I had felt that life had become meaningless, till I realized Rahul's presence, and that gave meaning and direction to my life. The past seven years saw me busy with Rahul, seeing him grow from moment to moment.

He was an extension of me, as I'm sure all children are of their mothers, but somehow, as a single parent, I was much too much invested in my son, mentally and emotionally.

I now began attending my mother-in-law's court regularly, and for longer periods of time. In fact, Queen Pajapati initiated me into counselling women, and I seemed to be able to help them get over their painful issues quite efficiently.

Once, a poor woman named Soma insisted that since she had lost her daughter to disease, and her husband had left her, she should also be allowed to live in the palace, like Kisa. This was a tough one to resolve.

I explained with immense patience that Kisa had been taken on as a companion by the Queen and not given refuge because she had lost her son. In any case, it was an emotional decision on the part of my mother-in-law, who believed that the monk Kisa met was her son Siddharth. Keeping Kisa with her was like keeping a part of Siddharth with her.

'Our purpose here is to learn to live life with others and not run away from it. I felt the same when my husband left. I thought my pain to be the greatest. Then I started listening to the stories of other women and realized I was not unique in my suffering. In fact, my problem seemed embarrassingly small compared to what others were facing. This jolted me back to reality. I also realized that my enduring could perhaps help another person to endure, just the way I was helped by listening to others' stories. That was a huge breakthrough in my life, and I've never looked back since.'

Soma seemed to understand my logic. The other women in the court also started telling her how the shared communion had changed their lives. All in all, things worked out in the woman's head, and that's what mattered.

Time and again, I had seen that accumulating information or knowledge did not transform us. Discourses, teachings, sermons were just words. They meant nothing till they were understood, assimilated and converted into wisdom. It was like food. Unless digested and absorbed by our body, whatever we ate would be of no use. Once absorbed into our system, the food can help in the growth and development of our body.

Transformation came through awareness. It came from absorbing and living that information, by understanding the experience. Transformation was essentially experiential. And every time a woman opened up in the court, she became aware and went back a transformed person. It was gratifying, indeed, to see the women being helped so.

At the end of such a busy but fulfilling day, I would look forward to spending time with myself and my plants. Narayani was also an enthusiastic gardener, reminding me of my grandmother at times.

Whenever I discovered a wild plant growing amongst the vegetables, I tended to pluck it out, assuming it to be a weed, but not Narayani. She replanted those weed-looking plants in another patch of land. Some of them were actually medicinal, like the short bright-green plants with tiny yellow florets, which turned out to be arnica, a potent painkiller.

According to Narayani, the earth grew nothing without

a reason. In the larger picture, every living or non-living thing had a purpose for their existence. What was this if not awareness!

While pottering about with plants, I stumbled upon an interesting phenomenon.

Narayani plants seeds in shallow trays, and once the saplings come up, we plant them wherever we want. Once I put an orange sapling to grow in a stone pot, just to see if we could grow small trees in pots, and then replant them later in a larger patch of land. To our surprise, the tree grew well in the pot.

Narayani suggested replanting it in a bigger place. 'If you want to eat oranges, then let it spread out and grow properly in a field. The poor tree will die in this pot.'

I resisted. I wanted to see if I could get oranges from the potted tree. Wonder of wonders, the orange tree did not die. It continued to grow. One day, I saw tiny white buds appearing in clusters on the little tree's branches. Narayani couldn't believe her eyes. Soon the tree was full of flowers. Eventually, most of the flowers turned into tiny oranges. We had created a dwarf orange tree in a pot! The tree looked the same as a normal tree, except that everything about it was small.

I learnt a very important lesson from this adventure of ours. We may try as much as we want, but we can only diminish the size of a plant by constricting its area of existence. But, and here is the learning, we cannot change the basic nature of that plant. It will do what it was born to do.

Eventually, the roots of our dwarf orange tree cracked

the stone pot, and we had to replant the tree on open land. It clearly showed that when the tree had exhausted all nourishment from the soil of its pot, it needed to get out, it had to break free. The pot and its soil were no longer enough for the orange tree's further growth.

King Shuddhodhan tried to restrict his son for twenty-nine years. Ultimately, Siddharth broke free.

What if I apply this analogy to my life? Why didn't I feel the need to break free? The answer was easy enough. I never felt restricted. Though I was tied up in various relationships within my family, those bonds were my support system, not my fetters.

In the end, it's all in our mind, isn't it!

The evenings stretching into nights seemed longer, now that there was no Rahul to chit-chat with. He had so much to tell me every day, so many questions to ask, and so many things to discuss. The absence of his chatter had created a silence in my life, but my mind was still full of the noise of our endless repetitive conversations.

One evening, as I sat watching the moon rising and the night becoming silent, I slipped into a beautiful space within my own self. There, I saw myself in many of my former lives, one overlapping the other…it was an exhilarating experience no doubt, but also revealed the impermanent nature of life, my own and everyone else's. Whether they were visions or just dreams of a bored mind, I'm not sure, but they seemed very real.

In one of these visions, I saw myself as an ironsmith's daughter. One day, in the market I bumped into a rich nobleman's son. He was Siddharth. Unknown to me, he fell in love with me and declared to his family that he wanted to marry me and no other. The family was aghast, as a nobleman marrying an artisan's daughter was unheard of. Nevertheless, Siddharth's father approached my father to request my hand in marriage with his son. To his great shock, my father refused outright, saying that Siddharth was not skilled in any craft, and hence unfit to marry me. Siddharth was not discouraged. He worked hard and learnt to make fine iron needles. Once he had mastered the craft, Siddharth approached my father with a bunch of fine needles to prove his eligibility as a suitable bridegroom for me. Duly impressed, my father agreed to the match. Thus, we were married.

This vision amused me as I was reminded of my father getting Siddharth to show off his skills in archery and debate, in various contests, just before our marriage. My mother had told me much later, after my marriage, that my father was quite sceptical about Siddharth being right for me as a husband. He felt that Siddharth was too soft a person and incapable of protecting me, let alone his kingdom. Interestingly, my father-in-law felt the same, and hence decided to hold the series of contests. Of course, Siddharth proved everyone wrong by winning all of them effortlessly.

Intriguingly, in none of the visions or dreams did I see myself as a subservient wife to a powerful dominating husband. I always saw myself as equal to my husband, as an equal part of a whole. In one of my dream-visions, I even saw myself as a ferocious lioness, living in a dense forest. All the wild animals of that forest tried to court me by strutting about or with mating calls and generally showing off. But I was attracted only to the majestic lion, the king of the animals. That lion of course was Siddharth.

Some might, at this point, say that I was obsessed with Siddharth, and hence saw these hallucinatory dream-visions. Well, maybe I was. And maybe all these dreams or visions were created by my fertile mind. Whatever the case might be, the one thing that I knew for sure was that these visions helped me tremendously in understanding the impermanence of life. They helped me in letting go of my familial bonds.

I could let go of my son.

I perceived the origin of my suffering to be within me. It was my attachment to my son, and the associated expectations or desires which were unfulfilled that caused me pain. I resolved not to allow these emotional cravings to pull me down and break me as they nearly did when Siddharth left.

I recalled my mother explaining to me how I was holding on to my memory of Siddharth as the person I had loved and married, and had expectations from. He had outgrown that role, as had my son. People grow, they evolve all the time, and like any living thing, they need to be unfettered for their growth to reach its natural peak.

Rahul had left because he had found his path. My job now was to bless him that he should find his destiny and be happy. Our children do not belong to us. Nobody belongs to anybody. Even our body does not belong to our spirit, it is just a temporary abode for one lifetime. Though seemingly a bit drastic, the thought of impermanence, and its understanding, was very comforting.

Once I was free of my emotional familial bonds, I discovered that my mind had fallen silent. The noise of expectations had disappeared. I was able to reflect. I was not absorbing anything. Remaining unaffected, I was behaving like a mirror, reflecting everything, and moving on from one moment, one reflection to another. Nothing bound me. I was free.

Gradually, my world changed, as I changed…the sunrise–sunsets looked different, as did the moon, stars and clouds in the sky. The flowers smelt different, and even the birds sounded more melodious.

I watched. I witnessed.

When I went for my walks, I would see not only the path, but even the pebbles on the way…some jagged, others rounded through years of wear and tear. I would see little leaves peeping out of crevices in stone walls, where the birds or the wind had carelessly dropped seeds. I noticed the new leaves and buds blooming in the plants and trees that were all around me. Then, there were birds collecting twigs to build their nests on high tree branches, and earthworms wriggling out of the wet flowerbeds, not forgetting the spiders weaving their intricate webs across the corners where the high walls of my rooms joined the ceiling.

I saw things I had never seen earlier and realized there was so much going on in the world around us that we habitually overlooked or just ignored.

I noticed that my senses had become heightened. I could hear the gurgling of water in the fountains from afar, as I could hear the footsteps of anyone approaching my rooms. I could smell the fragrance of freshly blooming flowers even before stepping into the gardens. It was as though the entire universe had suddenly opened up in front of me, in all its mesmerizing splendour.

My little vegetable garden showcased the dynamic nature of life, in its endless rhythmic cycles of generation, degeneration and regeneration in tune with the weather cycles. Everything in nature was so beautifully choreographed.

One morning, while walking, I meandered over to the peacock garden. It was King Shuddhodhan's favourite garden. His first wife, Siddharth's biological mother Queen Maya, was very fond of flowers and got them from all across the country. The peacock garden was created by her, and the plants tended by her personally. The royal peacocks strutted about happily in this exotic garden, lending it its name. The king considered the garden to be a living shrine to his dead wife and spent his mornings there.

Normally, one would find King Shuddhodhan in good humour in his favourite garden, but I found him looking dismal and sick, slouching in the bamboo gazebo that he had lovingly built in memory of Queen Maya. Though Siddharth had mentioned that the king did not have much time, I was fairly certain that he was not unwell. So I went up to him to find out what was ailing him.

'When Siddharth abandoned us, it caused me great pain. But then, he also took away his son whom he had left in his place. This loss is more than I can bear. It has cut through the skin straight to the marrow...'

The king was suffering indeed.

'Father, I understand your pain, as I went through it too. And I believe you made Siddharth promise not to ordain any youngster in the future, without the permission of his parents. You did right. You saved a number of families from this pain that you're going through. This is the quality of a great king—to think of the welfare of his subjects even when he himself is suffering.'

My response cheered up the king a bit.

'I know that your love for Rahul is making you grieve, and that you are upset with Siddharth. But, if you can loosen the tight bonds of this love and, with it, its strands, and embrace all fellow beings, then you will also understand what your son Siddharth stands for, as I have understood.'

My father-in-law did not respond, but I knew I had planted a seed in his mind. Leaving him in his cocoon of contemplative silence, I walked away towards the rose-apple tree, a landmark tree in Siddharth's life, which had now become my favourite too. Sitting under it transported me to the time Siddharth and I had spent together, soon after our marriage, exploring the gardens as well as each other.

I could, and actually did, spend hours talking to the tree as though it were Siddharth. Somehow I felt that my words did reach him wherever he was... I don't think anyone saw me talking seemingly to myself, but if they had, they would have surely questioned my sanity.

That day, a family of magpies was making quite a racket playing about the slender branches of the tree. The spike-petal magenta flowers were in bloom and probably driving the birds crazy. The long tails of the black-and-white magpies bobbing up and down furiously, while they chirped loudly all at once, was an amusing sight to behold.

Nevertheless, I sat down on my regular patch of grass, not disturbing the birds as I knew they wouldn't disturb me.

Since the tree was a favourite of the prince, the royal gardeners had landscaped the entire area such that it seemed to perch on a small mound, separating the gardens from the royal farms. Sitting under it, one could see the agricultural lands receding into the distant groves of fruit trees, beyond which lay the dark woods and lofty mountains. The gardens on the other hand stretched like a thick green carpet, all the way up to the main palace.

My back resting against the slim trunk of the rose-apple tree, I looked at the dark outline of the forest where the fields ended. My eyes were caught by the distant speck on a faraway field, which I assumed to be a farmer. Watching him move across the vast expanse of land, I was slowly lulled into my world of visions.

I saw a magpie, a deer and a turtle playing in the forest. As they frolicked, the deer got caught in a net. This meant that there was a hunter around somewhere. The deer told his friends to escape while they still had time. They refused as they didn't want to leave their friend behind.

The magpie told the turtle to start cutting into the ropes of the net that had trapped their friend, and herself flew around to check on the hunter. Soon enough, she found him walking along the path leading to where he had set the trap. She attacked the hunter on his head. Since she was small, she couldn't cause any harm to the burly man, except irritate him. She kept on attacking the man on his head, back, arm, leg, everywhere, till he yelled at her in anger, 'I am going to catch you and then wring your little neck, you pesky bird!'

The magpie continued to tease the hunter till he gave up, tired. That was enough. During this time, the turtle had managed to chew enough ropes to free the deer. The magpie's stalling of the hunter worked. The deer hobbled away as fast as he could, just before the hunter reached the trap. This angered him further, and seeing the turtle trying to slip away, the man pounced on him. The slow-moving turtle was caught easily. Seeing this, the magpie started to chirp loudly.

Suddenly, the hunter spied the deer peeping from behind the trees. He dropped the turtle and rushed after the deer. He must have assumed that an injured deer could be caught now, and the turtle, in any case, was an easy catch at any time. The deer led the hunter deep into the forest, giving the turtle enough time to make his escape. The ever-watchful magpie chirped loudly yet again. Hearing her, the deer bolted. The hunter returned to the trap only to discover that the turtle had also escaped.

The three friends had saved each other's lives. They had formed a sort of a circle where small or large, strong or weak, slow or fast was irrelevant—the only thing relevant was their will to help each other. It was a circle of hope, of compassion, of life.

I saw myself as the magpie, Siddharth as the deer, and Queen Pajapati as the turtle.

The cool breeze caressing my cheeks brought me back to the real world. The magpies had left. As I walked down towards the palace, I felt grateful to whoever that was sending me these visions. They were enlightening and somehow empowering. Looking around, one could easily comprehend that the circle of life was how nature functioned. It was right there in front of our eyes all the time.

The leaves fall off the trees every autumn and enrich the soil, helping other plants and grass to grow. The birds carry seeds from plants and trees and drop them elsewhere to grow. The bees go around collecting nectar from flowers and pollinating them in the process. Silently, the entirety of existence functions symbiotically like one big family, a huge circle of life.

Our lives had fallen into a without-Rahul routine, with everything the same as before except that King Shuddhodhan had started sharing his royal duties with Queen Pajapati. One would see more and more of the queen taking decisions and giving orders rather than the king. The responsibility of handling the queen's personal court, therefore, fell to me.

The number of women attending the queen's court was swelling by the day. In order to cope, we started meeting twice a day, morning and evening. Kisa was a great help. In fact, she made herself available twenty-four hours. So, the ladies who attended my court were kind of vetted and filtered by Kisa.

One day, as I was walking through the gardens, I heard Kisa's voice. She was sitting in a circle with five other women.

'Look around yourself. See the earth or fire, or even the air or water for that matter. Observe how they absorb, burn, blow away or dissolve whatever enters them, and yet their own basic elemental nature remains unchanged. Be inspired by them. Do not allow anything to change you. Happiness, pain, grief are parts of our lives. We cannot avoid them. What we can do is make them disappear within us, leaving us unaffected.'

The women seemed to be soothed by Kisa's soft, gentle voice and kind wise words.

I walked up to them. Kisa made a place for me to sit beside her and invited me to join in. The women continued to talk, and I just listened. Kisa called this a circle of hope. According to her, pain was real but so was hope.

I had mentally divided my feelings into pleasant, unpleasant and neutral. All of them were rooted in our mind and body, arising and passing away eventually. The important thing was to look for the source of those feelings. Anger, for instance, is mostly a reaction to something someone has done that is obviously not to our liking. So, if someone is angry with us, rather than responding to them with anger, we need to explore the cause, find out what we have done to warrant such a reaction. Because if we also react similarly, then the chain of reactions will go on forever. Better it is to uncover the cause. If we find our own conduct to be responsible, then we should be at peace. In case we are not at fault, then also, instead of retaliating, we should try to find a way to help the other person understand the situation and clear their misunderstanding.

We can thus be free from the bonds of suffering by understanding its nature, by just being aware.

I was fairly certain that all unpleasant feelings were due

to an incorrect perception of reality. We tend to see with our own eyes only; we must learn to see from others' eyes as well. It is a matter of tweaking our perceptions a little and the results can be magical. We were seeing that magic happen daily in Queen Pajapati's court, as I still preferred to call it, though she was unable to attend any more.

One day, we had a very interesting visitor in the court. This woman, Sumana, had come all the way from Rajgriha to meet me.

She had been to the Palm Forest, on the outskirts of Rajgriha, where Siddharth and his sangha resided during monsoon. She was deeply impressed at hearing Monk Kondanna talk about the Buddha. Yes, he was the same Kondanna who had predicted the possibility of Siddharth following a spiritual path. Subsequently, Sumana was lucky to get a chance to hear Siddharth himself, when he and his sangha were invited to meet the people of Rajgriha in King Bimbisar's court.

'All of us were eager to listen to this extraordinary man whose radiance illuminated even the people standing or sitting next to him. We wanted to know what secret had he discovered, and if we could do the same to become like him,' Sumana started narrating.

'There were also hundreds of children there, along with young Prince Ajatshatru. So the Buddha decided to tell us a story, as it was the best way to teach, he said.'

Thousands of years ago, a plumeria tree grew next to a lotus pond. There were no fish in this pond, though a short distance away, there was a shallow pond full of fishes and shrimps. A wicked heron flying overhead saw the two ponds, one with only lotuses and the other crowded with fishes and shrimps. His devious brain started working. The heron flew down and stood at the edge of the shallow pond, appearing to be deep in thought. After a while, a fish asked him what he was looking so grim about. The heron responded that there was a clean lotus pond nearby that had not a single fish living in it, whereas the pond where he stood was muddy and full of so many fishes and shrimps. It was so unfair, he said. The fish was tempted and wanted to visit such a heavenly pond herself.

The devious heron offered to take the fish in his beak. So, away they flew to the lotus pond. The fish was impressed. They went back to the old shallow pond, where the fish told everyone what she saw. Naturally, they all wanted to go to the lotus pond now. This is exactly what the heron wanted.

On the pretext of transferring the fishes from one pond to another, the heron would pick up a fish, and instead of dropping it into the lotus pond, take it to the plumeria tree to kill and eat it. Like this, slowly the fishes of the shallow pond were eaten up by the heron. He even ate up all the shrimps. A huge pile of bones and shells collected at the base of the plumeria.

Finally, one crab was left at the shallow pond. The heron offered to take him too. Since it was a big crab, the heron could not hold him in his beak. The crab had to ride on the heron's neck. Now this crab was smart. The moment the heron slowed down near the plumeria tree, the crab saw the pile of bones and understood what must have happened.

Angry to learn that all his friends were deceitfully eaten up by the heron, the crab dug his sharp claws into the heron's neck and squeezed. The angry crab kept on squeezing till the heron died and fell near the plumeria tree, where all the bones and shells of his victims lay. The crab crawled into the lotus pond.

In this story, the plumeria tree was the Buddha in one of his past lives, witnessing the wicked heron's actions and their ultimate consequence.

According to Sumana, the Buddha as plumeria in that life took a vow that since, as a tree rooted to the ground, he was unable to help the poor fishes and shrimps, in his subsequent lives he would strive to help all living creatures.

On hearing this, King Bimbisar gifted the Buddha a 100-acre bamboo forest called Venuvan to the north of Rajgriha. The monks and the people of Rajgriha worked together to build a monastery there, consisting of bamboo huts and prayer halls. The king and queen visited the Buddha daily. One day, Queen Videhi expressed her desire to be ordained like a monk. The Buddha refused, saying the time was not right for women to join the sangha.

'I have come to you in the hope that you might be able to convince the Buddha to accept us women into his sangha,' Sumana concluded.

'Why do you think he will listen to me?' I asked, touched by Sumana's faith in me.

'You were married to him, Your Grace. You know him best. I feel you would be able to impress upon him that women's needs are the same as men's.'

There was so much innocence in Sumana's words, in

her entire demeanour that I got up and hugged her on impulse.

'You are right, Sumana, I know him best, I understand him best. And the beauty of that understanding is that I know that he will do things when he thinks they should be done. Be sure, women will join the sangha one day.'

Whether Sumana was satisfied or not with my assurance, I wasn't sure, but yes, I was sure about women being in the sangha, one day soon.

Meanwhile, as the seasons changed and the months rolled into years, King Shuddhodhan slowed down physically, though mentally he was more active than ever. He would still give advice to Queen Pajapati and his council of ministers, as and when they needed it.

The queen was proving to be quite an efficient ruler, a fact that indirectly helped in the overall growth of the people of Kapilvastu. The girls suddenly became more active and started learning the subjects that were hitherto taught to boys only. Queen Pajapati had unknowingly become a role model for all the girls and women of Kapilvastu.

I must mention here that the culture and social norms of those times were not particularly favourable for women. The girls were married off young, they were not educated, and widows were cast away by their own families. I was very fortunate that all the women in my family were progressive.

Earlier it used to be my grandmother telling me stories about powerful women in the scriptures, now it was my mother-in-law who started doing the same.

'Did you know there were more than two dozen women who were learned *rishika*s, blessed with divine vision to write the hymns of the Rigveda?' The queen asked me during our meal one evening.

'Grandma mentioned only Lopamudra, who was a princess but married a sage and turned out to be smarter than him and wrote many hymns... I didn't know there were so many more,' I recounted, having a faint memory of hearing such a story.

'There were many more...Aditi, Urvashi, Indrani, Yami, Gosha, and so on. Our *rishi*s, the seers of those times, respected women as equals and exhorted people to do the same. Rishikas like Gargi and Maitreyi were more knowledgeable than most sages of their times. In fact, Gargi openly debated with men and was known to challenge the toughest of scholars, who eventually started avoiding her. She was one of the nine jewels of King Janak of Mithila's royal court.'

The very thought of elderly sages avoiding a young Gargi made me laugh.

'Those were ancient times, Mother. Over the centuries, things have changed completely...as we keep witnessing every day in your royal court,' I added sadly.

'Promise me, Yasho, that you will look after the women who come to seek help, our help. Whatever may happen, the court must continue functioning even after you and I have left. It is a very small but significant step that we have taken, and I am sure you also must have noticed its ripple effects.'

Pajapati held my hand affectionately, though her eyes were already lost in seeing something unseen...maybe a brighter future for the women of the land... Maybe. At least that's what I suspected from her smile.

The queen seemed to be imbued with the spirit of our ancient rishikas. I promised to carry forward her legacy.

Everything ran smoothly for a couple of years, till my father-in-law decided that he had accomplished what he was born to do, and that he would like to meet his son one last time to bid farewell. He had been through eighty-two autumns, and didn't want to go through this one.

The rainy season passed and autumn had just begun. This meant that the Buddha must be about to move or maybe had already moved from Vaishali.

King Prasenajit of Kosal was the latest in the line of Siddharth's ardent disciples, and we had heard that the entire royal family was listening to and following the Buddha's teachings of practising awareness and compassion. There was a story that was doing the rounds that time... I later realized that the Buddha mostly spoke through stories... somewhat like my grandmother.

The story went like this:

King Prasenajit's beautiful daughter Suprabha was of marriageable age, and her doting parents were looking for a suitable match for her. The king wanted his prospective son-in-law to be wealthy and powerful like him. He would tell his daughter that whatever love and respect she got from people was because she was his daughter, she was the princess of Kosal.

Suprabha disagreed. She said that she got only what she deserved, no less or more. She firmly believed that she was the architect of her destiny, not her parents. Her own deeds decided her fate, not her father's.

An angry Prasenajit had Suprabha married off to a

beggar. It turned out that the beggar once belonged to a rich family of Sravasti that had fallen into bad times and lost everything. On Suprabha's insistence, he took her to the ruins of his old family house. As they were looking around the dilapidated relic, they stumbled onto a chest full of gold coins, hidden deep below the rotting floorboards.

Within a few months, Suprabha and her husband had their house rebuilt, and the adjacent gardens restored to their former glory.

Though King Prasenajit was happy to see his daughter well settled, he wanted to know how this could have happened, and asked the Buddha.

Siddharth agreed with Suprabha that our own deeds pave our destiny, and told the King the story of Suprabha's past life.

It seems, many years ago, Suprabha was the chief wife of King Bandhumat. She was a kind-hearted lady and fed the beggars, the poor and the hungry whenever she got an opportunity. She also welcomed the mendicants passing through their city, offering them fresh warm meals. Initially, the king did not like all this, but eventually, he realized that the queen's actions were also making him very popular, not only in his own kingdom but the neighbouring ones too.

Those past good deeds of Suprabha had borne fruit in this life too. This was a fascinating revelation to Prasenajit. I am sure there were other such stories that Siddharth the Buddha would have shared with the king of Kosal and his family.

In fact, Siddharth had spent his last monsoon in Sravasti, the capital of Kosal, during which time a number of the lowest of lower caste men were also ordained into his sangha. This understandably made a certain faction of the people uncomfortable.

Our society was split into four castes, out of which the Brahmins were considered the most superior, as they were the learned ones. They deciphered the scriptures for us and conducted the numerous religious rituals. It was as though they were our mediums to reach the gods.

Siddharth had, since childhood, no patience with scriptures and rituals anyway.

The next in the caste hierarchy were us, the rulers and warriors. We governed the land under advisement of the Brahmins. The next were the traders, who were mostly travelling across the lands to procure goods for us. They set up shops in the markets on lands rented from people like us.

On the bottom rung of the caste ladder were the workers, who were hired by us as well as the traders to do our menial jobs. Finally, there were those who collected our waste and disposed of it in the designated places, on the outskirts of the towns or villages. These poor people were the outcastes. They travelled in the dark, keeping away from others, because it was believed that even the shadow of an outcaste could sully a person.

Siddharth was breaking these age-old divisions. On being questioned, he had apparently stated, 'We are all equal human beings. Every person's blood is red. Every person's tears are salty.'

Till today, I can never tire of admiring my husband's ability to instantly reduce everything down to its basic, simple components.

This inclusivity was a great political strategy as well, which, if followed by a monarch, could eliminate social tensions. I wasn't sure if any of the kings would go as far, but one thing was certain: the Buddha's sangha would swell immensely once the outcastes joined it. It was a far-sighted thought and would go a long way in teaching universal compassion to the world.

My Siddharth did me proud indeed. He was obliterating not only boundaries of caste but also those separating the various kingdoms. He was turning out to be a great ruler after all…he had begun ruling the hearts of people.

A messenger was sent to find the Buddha and relay King Shuddhodhan's request to him. And I knew that life was going to change for all of us, yet again.

9

FAREWELL

It had been four years since Siddharth the Buddha had visited Kapilvastu. This time I felt nothing, actually nothing, about his impending visit.

I was sitting under the rose-apple tree when Rohini came looking for me. 'The Buddha has arrived. He is with His Majesty now.'

'I am glad he came. It was important for the king to find peace before leaving his mortal body. I'm sure father and son will have a lot to talk about,' I smiled as I visualized them talking. It would be more of the father talking and the son listening this time, I reckoned.

Rohini was surprised at my reaction, and at my lack of interest, to say the least. How things had changed! Propriety stopped her from chiding me.

'You say this tree is like the Buddha for you when you talk to it. Now that he is here himself, don't you want to meet him face to face?' She put her concern across as politely as she could.

I laughed. 'Siddharth is within me; he is in every breath I take, in every drop of my blood. I don't need to meet him face to face. And when I talk about this tree, I am trying to say that I feel Siddharth's presence here more intensely than anywhere else, because of certain associated memories, nothing more. And no, I don't miss him like I did till four years ago, to answer the question that is bothering you so much,' I added with a gentle smile.

Flushing with embarrassment at having been caught, Rohini went back to the palace looking a bit flustered.

It was true; the Buddha permeated my surroundings as much as me, as I was a part of the whole. Meeting his physical form was irrelevant to me now. But I went down to the palace anyway, more to be with my father-in-law than anything else.

As he lay in his high-backed gilded bed, King Shuddhodhan looked pale, frail and much older than his eighty-two years. Siddharth was sitting by the bed with his father's hand clasped in his. Rahul, Anirudh and Anand stood close by.

'How time flies…it seems just yesterday when you were a toddler and loved to ride on my back. You grew up to be an exceptional student, and I saw a monarch in you…today, as you sit in front of me, I can admit how short-sighted I was…' the king paused to catch his breath.

Siddharth motioned to Rahul to hold the king's other hand, and said, 'The old leaves fall off the branch of the tree and new ones sprout, and the tree continues. Likewise it is with life. The temporal body arises from the four elements, which dissolve only to endlessly recombine again. So Father, you will continue to live in me and Rahul.'

My father-in-law looked unafraid and content, having

understood his son's words. Yet, he continued in a feeble voice, 'I dreamt of you as a great warrior, a great king ruling over not only the Shakyas, but maybe a few more neighbouring kingdoms as well. You became the greatest warrior of all and a ruler of not only our people but the entire country. You outgrew all my expectations, my dreams...you went way beyond.'

'The astrologers didn't see that there was only one path for you, not two. This path, this journey of yours was made in heaven, and I feel blessed that I had a small role to play in it. I die as a happy and proud father...seeking your forgiveness for all the wrongs that I did to you...' King Shuddhodhan's voice trailed off.

His hands held by his son and grandson, with a beatific smile on his lips, the King closed his eyes and passed on from this life. Siddharth gently folded his father's hands on his chest and announced his father's demise to the gathered ministers.

I walked away from there to the peacock garden. Sitting there in my father-in-law's favourite bamboo gazebo, I cried. The flow of tears seemed unending, as the pent-up grief of losing my mother and father combined with that of losing another father. I don't know for how long I cried, but when the tears finally stopped, I felt an immense lightness.

I got up to head towards my rooms but decided to take a longer route, as I knew the palace would be teeming with people—preparations for the funeral, and succession, and whatever else, had to be taken care of, which I was sure my mother-in-law would be handling with her usual calm efficiency.

I had no role to play in it.

As I started walking through the myriad royal gardens towards my side of the palace, it occurred to me that I saw Rahul as dispassionately as I did his father. I had noticed that he looked tall for his eleven years, his eyes were restless, yet, in his ochre robes, he seemed at ease and gelled well with the rest of the monks. Our eyes had met briefly, ever so briefly, when I entered the room, and then his attention was diverted to his dying grandfather.

And no, I was not angry or upset with him or his father; it was just that I was now in possession of my own life.

I was aware that all my suffering in the past was self-created due to my own anger and frustration at the non-fulfilment of my expectations. Once I faced my issues, I saw that Siddharth and Rahul had chosen their paths on their own, or maybe saw where their destinies lay. They had the strength of mind to follow that, and I was being selfish in wanting them to stay on with me, and to what end? Just to give me a few moments of happiness—happiness that was as ephemeral as a soap bubble!

The very cause of my selfishness was my unawareness of the larger picture. I was unconscious then, I was conscious now. I understood the source and nature of my suffering, and in doing that, became free of it. My unfettered heart was now full of wonder—wonder at the beauty of existence, of nature, of everything!

The funeral took place seven days later. Five hundred white-clad Brahmins conducted the funeral rites, while five hundred ochre-clad monks chanted. Siddharth circumambulated the funeral pyre thrice before lighting it.

His cousins Mahanama, Anirudh, Anand, Devdutt, Baddhiya and Kimbil stood behind him in support and deference.

Once lit, the crackling flames consumed the sandalwood pyre as the gongs and drums sounded to celebrate King Shuddhodhan's successful life and smooth transition into the heavenly realms. The people of Kapilvastu attended in great numbers to see the Buddha light his father's pyre.

Siddharth's cousin, the king's eldest nephew, Mahanama was unanimously selected as the heir to the throne. When his brothers and cousins left the palace to follow the Buddha, Mahanama had stayed behind. It was the smart thing to do, I suppose, as he was next in line to the royal throne of the Shakyas.

King Shuddhodhan had desired that our summer palace be given to Siddharth and his sangha, so they would have a place to stay whenever they visited Kapilvastu. Mahanama had efficiently seen to it that all arrangements were made accordingly.

Actually, once Siddharth left, I had felt no need for our three seasonal palaces. I had moved into the main palace with the king and the queen. It was better for Rahul to be with the family. The three palaces, therefore, lay vacant.

So, Siddharth and the monks stayed in the summer palace this time. During their stay, the feud between the Shakyas and Koliyas was brought to the Buddha's notice by Mahanama, who was worried about the imminence of war.

Siddharth's biological mother Maya was a Koliyan, as was Pajapati. The two kingdoms were tied by bonds of many royal marriages. They were practically one big family. Family infighting was understandable, but a war?

Let me digress a little…

Those days, the only way to have friendly relations amongst various kingdoms was to intermarry. The Shakya king Shuddhodhan's wives were the Koliyan princesses, the Magadh king Bimbisar's first wife Kosala Devi was Kosal king Prasenajit's sister, and so on. Marriage was considered a permanent glue for bonds lasting forever. What an irony! Here was Siddharth, who had walked away from his own marriage and was now helping two kingdoms resolve their embittered relationship.

Returning to war…that one should always go to the root cause of any suffering was something Siddharth had been preaching for a while, so he did just that. It turned out that the cause of trouble was shortage of water.

The water of Rohini River, which ran between the kingdoms of the Shakyas and Koliyas, was shared by both. For years now, rains had been sufficient, and Rohini's water had been more than enough for the crops. But in recent times, the population of both kingdoms had grown, and the surrounding forests were cut to increase the farmland. The water requirement had therefore increased as well, for which the farmers dug canals from the river to their fields.

Lately, maybe because of the lower rainfall, the streams and canals that fed the Rohini water into the farmlands were beginning to dry up. Frustrations on both sides made for an about-to-go-to-war situation.

Siddharth met the farmers on both sides and managed to convince them that human lives were more precious than water. They could sit together like a family to find a workable solution to their problem. He also told them that the breach between the two kingdoms could be taken advantage of by their bigger and stronger neighbouring kingdoms of Kosal and Magadh, who could easily take either, or both, under their control. Maintaining unity definitely made more sense.

Once again, Siddharth had managed to resolve an issue peacefully, while teaching the importance of compassion for fellow beings.

Since the Buddha and his monks were staying in the royal premises this time, my mother-in-law visited them frequently. On one such visit, she requested her son to take her along with him. She wanted to be ordained as a monk.

'In Rajgriha too, there are many women who desire to be ordained. The time is not right yet, to take on women in our sangha,' the Buddha rejected his mother's request, not just once but three times, till she gave up.

During that time, the monks led a tough life as they did not have any fixed place to live. They were constantly travelling on foot, begging for food once a day, and sleeping in the open at nightfall. A life not conducive for a queen, Siddharth must have thought.

But Queen Pajapati had actually not given up. Once the Buddha left Kapilvastu, she declared to all of us in her court one morning that she planned to leave everything behind and get ordained as a monk:

'I have done everything that I could as a queen. The new king will eventually bring a new queen. Considering we have created a new tradition of an all-women court, I'm sure the new queen will maintain it. As far as I'm concerned, I have decided to follow in my son and grandson's footsteps.'

'Didn't he turn you down earlier, Mother, when you asked him to ordain you?' I was a bit taken aback at her decision, given the history of her son refusing to allow her to join them.

'I am past the stage of worrying about what he will or won't say or do. I long for freedom and I am prepared to seek it, no matter the cost. Women are not inferior to men in terms of attaining enlightenment. The Buddha himself says that all humans are equal. He has accepted the untouchables into the sangha, so he should accept us women too.

'I would be happy to join the Buddha's sangha, but if he doesn't allow it for any reason, I would still follow him wherever he goes,' the queen's voice rang firm with resolution, quite like her grandson's from some moons ago.

As the news spread, a number of women decided to join my mother-in-law's quest. All of them shaved their heads and donned yellow cotton robes like the queen. At a pre-decided day, about fifty of them left their family, home, jewels and all material possessions, and congregated at the palace at sunrise.

Led by Queen Pajapati, the sangha of women walked out of the palace gates, and subsequently walked out of Kapilvastu. They were headed to the Licchavi capital Vaishali, as that's where the Buddha and his monks were staying at that time. It took them fifteen days to reach Vaishali on foot, as it was even beyond the kingdom of Koliya.

Looking back at that significant moment, and recalling Queen Videhi of Magadh, Sumana, and many others I didn't know then, I realize I have always felt that women are naturally gifted to attain spiritual heights, contrary to popular belief.

We absorb so much: we are told to remain strong for our children, so we pretend to be strong, quashing our inner turmoil, pushing it to the deep dark recesses in our hearts. We have no one, no place to go to in case we want to vent. Why? Because we are surrounded by people who want us to be emotionally strong. Eventually our tears dry up. I think that, in a way, makes it easy for us to tip over to the other side—detach ourselves from the material life, so to speak.

To put it forth more succinctly, since we are used to hiding our emotions, we might as well drop them, considering they are of no use to us. It's like possessing jewels but keeping them hidden from the world, not wearing them at all. Such jewels become useless and can be given away easily.

Queen Pajapati was available, whenever needed, as a pillar of strength to her sister, husband, son, daughter-in-law, grandson, and the numerous women of Kapilvastu and nearby areas. Who knew what was happening within that strong pillar! The time had come for her to spend the rest of her life with her own self, doing whatever her heart desired. The king's passing was her tipping point; she had slid over to the other side.

Channa, though living in his quarters in the palace compound, continued his visits to Anand. He was my source of information about Siddharth and Rahul, and now Queen Pajapati.

Channa reported that early one morning, Anand, while

going to the lake to fetch water, saw the lady monks sitting at the entrance of the monastery. He did not recognize them at first, as all of them had shaven heads. In fact, Anand assumed them to be a group of monks visiting from another kingdom. On closer look, he was shocked to see the queen amongst the group; she seemed to be their leader. Since they had walked hundreds of miles barefoot, all the ladies had swollen bleeding feet.

'Dear Anand, we have shaved our heads and given away all our fine clothes and jewels. Free from material possessions, we have left our homes and families too. We have been walking in search of the Buddha. It took us fifteen days to reach here. All through this time, I can assure you that we have followed your path; we slept by the roadside and begged for food once a day, in small villages along the way. Now we want to be formally ordained by the Buddha as monks. Please convey our request to him. Tell him that we women also go through old age, sickness and death, and deserve freedom from them, just like men do.'

Queen Pajapati wanted to be sure this time that the Buddha should see that the women were as fit and capable as men to become monks and follow his path. Since he had declined her outright when they last met at the palace, Pajapati wanted Anand to plead her case; and this time, her case seemed much stronger.

Earlier when they had met, at the time of King Shuddhodhan's death, Pajapati, though bereft of all jewels, was in the white silks of a royal widow. She approached her son as a widowed mother, who wanted to leave everything in search of peace. The compassionate Siddharth did not want his mother to go through the tough life that he had chosen. It was the reaction of a protective son. This time around, by placing Anand in their midst, Pajapati had cleverly removed the mother–son shackles. Her request was that of a woman representing all the women of the kingdom, nay the world.

Apparently, it took Anand some time to convince the Buddha, but he managed to do it eventually. The senior monks Sariputra, Mogallana, Mahakashyap and others conferred together to create special statutes for the women, which Pajapati happily accepted. The women were ordained monks, or nuns as they were called.

The idea was to be with the Buddha and follow his path, and it could be achieved only by becoming a part of his ever-growing contingent of monks. I am sure Pajapati was more than happy at finally being with her son, though the relationship now was that of student and teacher, rather than of mother and child.

Queen Pajapati managed to get a monastery built in Vaishali for the nuns and invited me to join them, to which I sent a polite refusal.

I had no intention of joining those women in following the Buddha. I was too busy paving my own path, and happy doing so. In my heart of hearts, I felt that being with Siddharth now would defeat our purpose—his as well as mine. My suffering had birthed my path, my very own personal path, one that no one, not even the Buddha himself, could walk on. I was not willing to abandon this path that had arisen, or rather co-arisen, alongside his.

News would keep coming to me through Channa, about how the Buddha's following was spreading to the lands I did not know about, and how his wealthy followers were building monasteries and rest-houses for the wandering monks.

The Venuvan bamboo forest monastery near Rajgriha was gifted by King Bimbisar of Magadh. The Jetavan monastery near Sravasti was built and gifted by Sudatt and Prince Jeta, son of King Prasenajit of Kosal. The Licchavi princes transformed a forest in Vaishali into a monastery. More and more monasteries of different sizes were cropping up wherever the Buddha's words were echoing.

The monks and nuns would walk all through the year, spreading the Buddha's teachings, and rest only during the three-month-long rainy season, for which the monasteries were being built. Like all of Siddharth's decisions, this was also a practical one, as the rains in our region brought forth snakes and other creepy-crawlies out of their abodes, converting the forest paths into dangerous terrain. My husband was always the pragmatic one in the family.

In fact, I realized more and more that Siddharth had never changed. His core nature remained the same...he just grew up, matured.

Once Pajapati became a nun, Siddharth sent many more aspiring women, whom he continued to meet during his travels, to her to be trained. Once, he was on a journey with Anand, and they stopped by the roadside to rest. They saw an old woman drawing water from a well. Siddharth asked Anand to get some water for him.

The moment the woman learnt who was asking for

water, she took the pitcher herself. On reaching the Buddha, she put the pitcher down and took him in her arms. A horrified Anand tried to stop her, but Siddharth motioned him to stay away.

Once done with embracing, the old woman gave water to both the men. Siddharth explained to Anand that the woman had been his mother for many hundred births and still carried that love for him. He then sent her to Pajapati.

This and more such stories were brought to me by not just Channa, but other women too, who came to meet me. After my mother-in-law's departure from the palace, though, the attendance of women at her court, which was being handled by me, dwindled—Kisa had also accompanied Queen Pajapati. I attended to the women as patiently as before, listening to their stories, telling them mine, and of others that I had heard over the years.

Sometimes, some women would just come to talk. They had no problems in their lives. It was just that they were restless, and now more so, since Siddharth had encouraged people to question everything. Queen Pajapati leaving her material life behind to seek freedom from suffering stood out as an example that such a step could be taken.

One such restless woman was Uttama. She had a tough yet interesting question.

'Your Grace, the other day I heard a young monk preaching that in love there is suffering. How is it possible? Love brings happiness; it cannot cause suffering. Without love, life would be empty of meaning. Are these monks learning all this from the Buddha?' Uttama looked baffled.

'Over the years I have learnt that there are some things

you should never ignore: a young prince, a small snake, a spark of fire, and a young monk. A young prince is destined to be a king, a small snake can kill a large man, a spark of fire can burn down a forest to ashes, and a young monk can be enlightened. Now, let's see what he meant by love causing suffering.'

My possessive streak had surfaced. A lot of people felt that Siddharth was too young to be the Awakened One. Whenever I got the chance, I would always make it clear to whosoever cared to listen that age had nothing to do with being enlightened. Siddharth had hundreds of young followers, and they carried his words to the people. It was unfair to judge them by their age.

'Yes, you are right, Uttama, love gives us immense happiness, but only when the object of love is with us. Love results in attachment. I am sure you would agree with me when I say that we are scared to lose whoever, whatever we are attached to, be it people or land or any other material things. We are always worried that no harm should befall our loved ones. Is this not suffering? And we certainly suffer when we finally lose our loved ones… No monk, young or old, has told me all this. I say it from my own experience,' I added.

'What is love then? Why are we taught to love if it is going to make us suffer?' was the inevitable follow-up from Uttama.

'Again, I will tell you what I learnt from my personal experiences. I believe love to be compassion, kindness and, most of all, understanding. Such love has no place for "me" or "mine". It is an all-encompassing love that makes the object of our love grow to its full potential. Such non-discriminatory love brings peace and happiness to all. Can you imagine what such universal love could do to the world? There would be no wars, no destruction of nature, no killing of animals…everyone co-existing peacefully as nature intended for us to do.'

I admit I was liable to get carried away when talking about this newfound understanding of mine, but I think I did manage to sow a seed in Uttama's mind that day.

In due course, a number of women started feeling that if the queen could leave everything to be with the Buddha, why not them! Gradually, the number of nuns following in Pajapati's footsteps started increasing.

By the by, with just a couple of women coming now and then, I had more and more time on my hands. I had started growing medicinal herbs and mushrooms in one part of the garden, close to the rose-apple tree. I had my grandmother's green fingers, and her instinct for understanding the usefulness of herbs in maintaining our body's internal balance. Narayani was always there as well, to guide me as she did with my vegetable patch.

Since I had more time now, I started visiting nearby villages. Either Rohini or Narayani would accompany me, and we carried fresh herbs with us. Every day I would find some or the other person who I knew could benefit from my herbs in their physical or even mental state, and they did.

I had unconsciously become a healer.

Suddenly the ebbing tide of women coming to my court reversed. Now, those with physical ailments started coming to me. Somehow, my herbs were helping them, and while treating their physical ailments, we realized that most of these issues were a result of their lack of mental well-being.

For instance, there was Manjula, who had a recurring skin rash that seemed unrelated to weather, food, clothes or anything else. Intuitively, I gave her herbs to calm down her entire system, including her mind—though outwardly she didn't look agitated at all. I also gave her some poultice for physical application. Finally, it was the herbal drink that resolved her problem. It also loosened her up enough to talk about her stresses in life. She had not conceived and was worried that her husband might get another wife.

There were many more Manjula-like women, who were quietly absorbing stress in their everyday life and falling prey to all sorts of aches and pains, digestive problems, sleep problems, skin and hair issues; some had even become bed-ridden with their muscles giving up completely. I was reminded of my days of a similar kind of suffering when my body gave up in rebellion on Siddharth's leaving me, and how my mother's decoctions helped me recover.

We tend to give too much importance to our mind, and the mind is full of noise, echoing the words of people around us, telling us what is right for us to do and what is not. The right and wrong, of course, is being decided by the people, the society, our families, neighbours, and so on. The noise of our mind drowns our consciousness, and we slip into a stupor. In fact, we sleepwalk our way through life, following the directions given by others via our mind.

When Siddharth left, my mind told me he had left me

and our baby. When I quietened the mind, it said Siddharth had left for the greater good of the people. The mind makes us selfish. It quickly fills up with all kinds of desires, hunger, greed, which if unfulfilled result in anger, creating further chaos in an already noisy mind.

The moment we shut off our mind, our natural alertness awakens. We begin to see nature in all its glory; we see how the universe really is one big family. We also see how far tender loving care goes and how it grows to encompass every living being it comes across. We see how our hearts connect.

Though my close family members were with me no more, I felt that my family had grown, grown exponentially… and continued growing.

I wasn't sleepwalking any more, I was wide awake. I was in a state of 'no-mind'.

10

THE SANGHA

One fine spring morning, Rohini was helping me string the coral jasmine flowers to wear in my hair. I had stopped wearing jewels long back, and also stopped using fragrances that I had loved once. I remember being exceptionally fond of exotic perfumes that were brought to our town by merchants coming from up north. How I looked forward to my seasonal jaunts to the market with my mother!

Coming back to the present, I had now become fond of wearing fresh flowers in my hair or wrists. I loved to collect the fallen flowers from the royal gardens, in the early morning, and wear them till they wilted by the evening. Their fragrance would last the entire day and give me intense happiness. It felt as though I had merged with nature or that nature was within me.

Rohini used to help me in collecting flowers as well as stringing them into ornaments. Her deft fingers could create necklaces or bracelets or even earrings out of any shape or size of flowers.

That morning Rohini had a question for me:

'When Her Majesty Queen Pajapati was leaving the palace, she said she wanted freedom. As I understood, she wanted freedom from old age, disease and death. But how is that even possible? Everyone grows old, most people fall sick, and we all die eventually.'

Rohini's confusion was quite reasonable.

'You are right, Rohini. One who is born has to go through sickness, old age, and finally has to die. Freedom is not from this, as this is the law of nature. Freedom is from our attachment to all these natural happenings. We get excessively attached to our youth and hate getting old, or falling sick for that matter. We accumulate so many possessions in our lifetime that we don't want to die for fear of losing them. The freedom that Queen Pajapati was looking for is the understanding of nature, the truth of life...the freedom from all attachments. Freedom is awareness, that's all.'

'Is that why you didn't leave? You are already free,' Rohini responded with a twinkle in her eyes.

'Maybe. Come, let's finish off this work before the flowers start wilting in impatience.'

This conversation with Rohini made me ponder. I really did feel free, though this word in the above context had not occurred to me till now. I was living in today, in the here and now, observing people and nature, with no thoughts of tomorrow...yes, that's how freedom felt, I suppose.

It seemed so long ago, when Siddharth left, when I realized the truth; when the finality of his action sunk in, every cell of my being had rebelled. I shivered in anger from the tips of my toes to the roots of my hair; it felt like a volcano bubbling inside me was ready to erupt and destroy everything in the blink of the eye. In that state of being so alive, I wanted to die.

Today too, I felt as alive as when I had wanted to die—but this time there was no volcano.

My grandmother used to tell me stories all the time. All those stories had something hidden in them, mostly a life skill to learn. Chatting with Rohini had triggered the memory of a story that my grandma told me, soon after my marriage was fixed with Siddharth. I was too excited then to pay much attention to the message in the story, as it seemed straightforward enough.

Today, nearly three decades later, as I recall the story, I think that my grandmother probably, intuitively, knew of my destiny. The story goes something like this…

Long ago, a young man named Sumedh lived in a small village in the kingdom of Divapati, at the Himalayan foothills. One day, he decided to go to the capital of the kingdom to study. He was clever and hardworking, and was confident of his success. The capital city was far away and those days common people would walk to their destination. So did Sumedh.

Since he was carrying just the bare essentials with him, Sumedh had to stop on the way and seek work to buy food and find shelter. He was quite successful in doing that, and by the time he reached the capital, he had actually saved up five copper coins.

When Sumedh entered the city, everyone seemed to be preparing for some celebration. Looking around, he spied a young girl holding a bunch of lotus flowers. 'What is the celebration today?' he asked. The girl's name was Sumitra.

'Today, the enlightened Master Dipankar is arriving in the city. The celebrations are in honour of him.'

Sumedh was happy to find this opportunity to meet an enlightened master. Maybe he could request him to be his teacher...the young boy's thoughts had started galloping. But he didn't have anything to offer to the Master. Turning to the girl, he asked, 'Can I buy some lotus flowers? How much did you pay for them?'

'I paid five copper coins for five lotus flowers. And two of them, I plucked from a pond on the way.'

'Can I buy five flowers from you? I will give you five copper coins for them.'

'How can I sell them? I bought them to gift the Master myself,' said Sumitra, incredulous.

'You will still have two flowers left, which you can gift. I have come from a distant village. It is a rare opportunity for me to meet an enlightened master. Hence, I would like to not only meet him but also request him to take me on as his student. So, please allow me to buy your flowers, and I promise to do anything you ask.'

Sumitra thought for a while. Then she said a very strange thing, 'I don't know what connection we have from our past lives, but the moment I saw you, I fell in love with you. I will give you these flowers to offer to the Master, but only if you promise me that in this, and in future lives, you will take me as your wife.'

Sumedh was understandably dazed. He quickly gathered his wits and responded, 'You are special indeed. But I want to seek the path to liberation. If I marry, I would not be free to follow my path.'

'You promise that I will be your wife, and I will promise that when the time comes for you to seek your path, I will not prevent you from going. On the contrary, I will do everything I can to help you in achieving your goal of liberation,' said young Sumitra, who seemed quite sure of herself.

Sumedh happily accepted the girl's proposal and together they went to meet Master Dipankar. The crowds were swelling by the minute, and the young couple could barely get a glimpse of the great Master. But that one glimpse was enough for Sumedh to decide that one day he would attain such enlightenment. Since it was impossible for them to reach any closer to the Master, Sumedh, on the spur of the moment, tossed the flowers towards him.

Miraculously, the flowers landed right in the hands of Master Dipankar. Sumitra asked Sumedh to toss her two lotuses too towards the Master. Sumedh did that, and they also landed in the Master's hands. Seeing this strange phenomenon, Master Dipankar asked the two to step forward. Sumedh held Sumitra's hand, and the crowd parted to make way for the couple to reach the Master.

As the young couple bowed in front of Master Dipankar, he blessed Sumedh, 'I see the sincerity of your heart. One day, in a future life, you will attain the enlightenment that you seek.' Then he turned to Sumitra and said, 'And you shall be his closest friend in this life and many lives to come. Just remember your promise to help your husband attain his goal.'

The young couple was overwhelmed and devoted themselves to studying under the great Master Dipankar. Many lives later, Sumedh became an enlightened Master himself, with his wife constantly supporting him.

Now, why my grandmother should narrate me this story was a riddle I could never solve. The learning I took from the story was to always be supportive of my husband. At that time, I thought of this story as one of many others, like that of Sita perhaps, teaching girls to be sensitive and understanding wives. And that was that.

Maybe my grandmother was preparing me for my destiny, because while recalling the story today, I felt very strongly that Sumedh was Siddharth, and I was the young Sumitra with lotuses.

You see, by now I was getting these thoughts or recollections of stories or even dreams which were very real and made me feel as though they were windows into my past lives, mine and Siddharth's. I was unable to separate the past from the present, or even the future; it seemed like one long saga to me—just one single story.

Weeks, months and years were rolling by, but for me, time was not divided any more…it was a flowing river, heading towards its destination, the sea.

After our chat about freedom the other day, Rohini spread the word and within the blink of an eye, women started flocking to meet me. I was not holding a court like Queen Pajapati anymore, so they would find me in the royal gardens, till I fixed a place where we could all sit on the grass and talk. It was a large patch of grass surrounded by orchards, beyond the rose-apple tree, towards the fields and the forest.

Inadvertently, I had created a sangha of women of all ages who wanted to be free while living with their families, within their homes.

Anand would also come by to visit, whenever he was passing through the city. He would regale me with stories of Rahul's efforts to follow the rules set for the monks, as well as tales of miraculous transformation of people through the Buddha's teachings, and sometimes, by his mere presence.

Rahul was a *sramaner* yet, a novice, and there were very few such young ones in the sangha. He was looked after by Sariputra, one of the elders, and treated like any other monk, not as the son of the Buddha.

After some years, another young boy called Svasti also joined the sangha. Rahul and Svasti became good friends. Svasti had met the Buddha when he attained enlightenment near the river Niranjana. He was an orphan and used to look after the buffaloes for a farmer in return for food and shelter. When Rahul came to know this, he wanted to meet the buffaloes in person, and possibly ride one. Maybe Svasti did manage to fulfil his friend's wish, or maybe not, one didn't know, but imagining Rahul riding a buffalo made me laugh out loud, with Anand joining in.

As a child, my Rahul was already precocious, so as an adolescent, I could well imagine how restless his brain would be. According to Anand, he once misled some royal guests by giving them wrong directions when asked about the Buddha. But such a prank was unacceptable.

Next day, Siddharth met Rahul and told him to get some water in his begging bowl. After washing his hands in it, he asked, 'Rahul, is this water good for drinking?'

Rahul's response was a prompt 'no'.

The Buddha asked Rahul to throw away the dirty water and asked if the bowl was good enough to eat food from.

'No, I would need to wash it first,' was Rahul's very sensible response, or so he thought.

Next, Siddharth took the bowl from Rahul and tossed it away. Rahul turned to look at his bowl, which lay awkwardly in a shrub next to his hut, wondering what the Buddha was possibly trying to tell him.

'Are you worried that the bowl might break?'

'No, it would not matter if the bowl gets damaged, as it's just a container to hold food.'

'Just as you don't care about this bowl, people won't care about you, Rahul. You started out as a clean bowl, but have started accumulating the dirt of lies and trickery. Remember, like this bowl, you will be cast aside and forgotten. Your goal of getting enlightened, for which you left a princely life, will not be fulfilled, as you have lost the way.'

This admonition, coming from his father, the Buddha himself, reformed Rahul completely. And I was glad that Siddharth did manage to play the role of father eventually; otherwise he had decreed that the sangha did not recognize familial relationships, just like it did not recognize caste and class. Everyone was equal as a human and was treated as such.

But…what they overlooked was that whatever rules anyone may make to run a sangha successfully, parenting follows its own rules. Parenting is a part of nature and nature's unfathomable rules are unbreakable, yes even by the

Buddha. Rahul was too young to join the sangha when he did. Anyway, with respect to King Shuddhodhan's request to Siddharth, children as young as Rahul were not taken into the sangha any more.

One afternoon, Anand came visiting from Sravasti. That rainy season, the retinue of 500 monks was residing in Jetavan, in a monastery built by Sudatt, a travelling businessman and an ardent follower of the Buddha.

It so happened that while they were residing there, they heard about a cold-blooded marauder terrorizing the people of Sravasti. He was nicknamed Angulimal, as he was fond of wearing garlands strung with the fingers of his victims.

Once the Buddha heard about this murderer, he set out to meet him, against all well-meaning advice of the monks, and even the townspeople. Anand, being the shadow of Siddharth, followed him.

According to the people of Sravasti, Angulimal lived in a cave, in the forest area at the edge of the city. So, Siddharth went looking for him there, from where no one had ever come back alive.

Anand followed. According to him, Angulimal was hiding behind a rock, but seeing an unarmed monk, he came out laughing.

'Armed men have come here, never to return. Yet, look at this foolish unarmed monk, who fearlessly walks this way!' So saying, the man brandished his gleaming knife.

The Buddha continued walking, without changing his pace, and walked past him, leaving the hardened criminal gaping in bewilderment.

Meanwhile, Anand could see the Buddha's figure receding, as Angulimal started to run after him. Strangely, almost miraculously, it seemed that the killer was unable to catch his prey.

'It looked as though the Buddha was running faster than Angulimal, yet he was just walking at his normal pace. And Angulimal, who was actually running, didn't seem to be able to cover much distance between himself and the Buddha!' Anand sounded flabbergasted himself, as he narrated wide-eyed and with animated hand gestures.

Finally, Angulimal had to shout, 'Stop, O monk, stop!'

The Buddha stopped and turned around. 'I stopped long back; it is you who has to stop now,' he said.

Neither Angulimal nor I could understand what the Buddha meant. He then slowly walked towards the man and explained, 'I have foresworn violence against all living beings, whereas you want to kill every living person you meet. This is what I mean when I say stop.'

By the time the Buddha reached Angulimal, the murderer was down on his knees, crying.

Thereafter the Buddha, accompanied by Angulimal and Anand, returned to the monastery.

'Angulimal has now become a monk with a shaven head and orange robes,' Anand ended the story with a flourish.

I recalled when Siddharth would feed birds and animals, they would actually come and peck or lick his hands. If the wild creatures could sense his compassion instinctively, I was sure, so could a wild man like Angulimal.

Compassion did make the world go round. It was his

deep-seated compassion for the fellow living beings of the world that made Siddharth leave a bunch of living beings at home, to go out in search of a resolution for the suffering of a much larger lot of living beings.

Mankind gained from our family's loss, but then that loss pushed us to look within ourselves, and at each other, understanding the power of shared compassion. It is true: for every gain there must be a loss, and from every loss emerges a great gain. We gained a larger family, the entire world.

'Seeing all these miraculous transformations, I wanted to be like the Buddha and transform the world, and I said so to him, once Angulimal joined our monastery,' Anand continued.

I knew Siddharth's answer to that already, yet I asked Anand anyway.

The Buddha responded thus, 'What is needed is for each person to be themselves and not copy me. Every individual is different and has his own level of understanding. First a person has to understand or acquire his own individuality, after which he has to give it up to attain enlightenment.'

The words spread a warmth of joy in my entire being, as they, yet again, reflected how in sync Siddharth and I were in our thoughts and understanding.

'Most rivers make their way to the sea. Once they merge with the expansive waters of the sea, the rivers shed their identities; they cease to be individual rivers. What we see is one vast water body, the sea. But then, there are some rivers that do not reach the sea. So is the case with us, Anand,' I explained.

I think he now understood what the Buddha meant.

'Devdutt is one such river that will not reach the sea,' Anand sighed.

'Why do you say so? It's unlike you to judge people!'

'No, no! Far be it from me to judge. The other day in Rajgriha, the Buddha was telling Devdutt that they were brothers and should be forgiving towards each other. But as usual, Devdutt scoffed. Later on, we asked the Buddha what the reason could be behind Devdutt's constant misbehaviour towards him.

The Buddha told us that this had been happening for many past lives. Then he told us a story.

In the past, in Benares, there was a king called Brahmadatt. His wife was Queen Durmati, and they had a son called Dharmapal. Durmati was short-tempered and vicious by nature. Once, as it happened in those times, and even now with some kings, Brahmadatt was enjoying himself in the company of many beautiful women. He was so happy that he sent some wine to the queen too, in an attempt to celebrate his happiness.

Queen Durmati felt insulted, maybe rightly so, at this gesture of her husband. But her reaction was quite extreme. She said that she would rather slit her son's throat and drink his blood than drink the wine sent by the king. Brahmadatt was no better. He called his son and informed him of his mother's desire.

Poor Dharmapal kept on pleading and crying that he was their only son and had never caused them any harm, so why should they treat him so! All in vain. The king slit his son's throat and gave the blood to his wife to drink.

King Brahmadatt was now Monk Kokalika, Queen Durmati was Devdutt, and Dharmapal was the Buddha in this life.

Though a part of the sangha, Kokalika had become a favourite of Devdutt, and helped in creating and spreading false rumours about the sangha and its members, as I learnt later.

'Devdutt's core nature has remained unchanged, even after joining the sangha. In fact, his jealousy has been increasing in the same proportion as the Buddha's popularity. This is one river that is surely running away from the sea,' Anand concluded.

Maybe he was right.

11

ALONE AGAIN

Life was flowing smoothly, routinely. Nearly two decades had passed since Siddharth's last visit to Kapilvastu.

King Mahanama, Siddharth's cousin, was ruling Kapilvastu as efficiently as his predecessors.

'We belong to the lineage of King Ikshvaku, one of the sons of Manu, the first human on earth!' He was proud of his lineage and felt duty-bound to carry it forward faithfully.

Occasionally, Mahanama would send word to his brothers that he wanted to meet them. He must miss them, I always thought, recalling our childhood days when all the cousins had fun playing and eating together. Though I had spent just a few years with them, once in a while I too felt nostalgic about those days and missed the camaraderie we shared.

Mahanama had lived with them…and was now alone, while the rest of them were still together, in a way.

Anirudh and Anand started visiting us whenever they got a chance. Initially, when either of them would come,

Mahanama would invite me to join them for a meal, a formality I dropped out of very soon.

Since Anand was close to me since childhood, he would always manage to find me in one of my various hideouts—as he loved calling them—while Anirudh and I met less often. If at all we met, it was not by design, but by unwittingly crossing each other's paths during his visits to his brother.

Coming back to Mahanama…in one of our meal-meetings, Anirudh sounded quite charged up.

Apparently, there was some infighting amongst the monks regarding the various duties they were supposed to perform. One monk forgot to do something that he was supposed to, the other reprimanded him for that. The first one claimed that it was not deliberate on his part, and that there was some misunderstanding or miscommunication amongst the monks, but the second one insisted that deliberate or not, it was still a misdemeanour and warranted punishment.

The entire incident escalated and created two opposing factions in the sangha, one for each monk. Clearly, the Buddha's teaching of compassion for fellow humans had been grossly overlooked by these monks. Finally, after days of intense discussion amongst the monks, the elders and the Buddha, a way to settle such disputes was arrived at.

'It was decided that no disputes would be discussed in private. They should be stated in public, in front of the sangha, so that both sides of the conflict are presented. Witnesses and evidence, if any, should be presented while narrating the problem in detail. Both the conflicting parties should confess to whatever they have done wrong, and accept their own faults. Once the sangha passes a collective verdict, it should be acceptable to both the parties,' Anirudh announced with a flourish.

'Oh yes, there would always be elders present in such meetings, to help the conflicting parties to move on, once the verdict is out,' he added.

'I agree. That's how the justice system should work,' I said. To my immense, now oft-repeated, pleasure, this way to resolve conflicts showcased Siddharth's skills as a ruler par excellence, yet again.

King Mahanama was listening to his brother's words with rapt attention. Undoubtedly, he would apply them as a ruler as well. Anirudh would often visit the king to share such gems from the Buddha. It was almost like Siddharth was ruling the Shakyas by proxy, through Mahanama. If my father-in-law were watching from the heaven above, I'm sure he would be pleased with the final outcome of how the kingdom was being ruled.

I was told that Siddharth's sangha was growing faster than any kingdom. The royal families supported him, and became lay followers of the Buddha. This reflected in an increase in the sangha members, because the followers of these kings, or their families, also became followers of the Buddha. Many men and women left their homes to become monks and nuns. The ones who didn't, remained lay followers, and waited for the Buddha to visit their town or village to hear him talk.

The ever-growing sangha needed more monasteries, which was taken care of by the wealthy followers of the

Buddha. For thousands of monks and nuns, many small and large monasteries cropped up everywhere—so much so that I lost count after a while.

As a mere observer, I would surmise that running a sangha or running a kingdom were much the same. Come to think of it, the smallest unit of it all, of people, was a family. To live harmoniously as a family, one has to share a common space with the others as well as the essentials of daily life like food, chores, or any other responsibilities.

Apart from this, one had to be careful not to hurt others with their words or deeds. Sharing personal insights along with respecting the others' viewpoints, and at the same time not imposing one's own on others, is yet another aspect of living peacefully within a family. Other than these very basic precepts, there were the usual etiquettes of respecting the elders, apologizing for mistakes committed, showing compassion to all, and so on.

What us women naturally learnt from the elders of our family was something that Siddharth was probably deriving from his observations of living in a sangha. He wouldn't have needed to do this had he lived a normal life like I did.

Actually, not only me, all women were brought up learning these basic precepts or etiquettes of living within a family peacefully, as a norm. The men were exempt. The reason behind this discrimination, according to my mother, was the fact that women entered new families on getting married, where they had to live the rest of their long lives. The prudent thing to do in such a case was to adjust within the new family as soon as possible, and for that the rules were laid out for us.

Siddharth lived amongst men. The monks must be as ignorant as him about these things. The nuns, who lived at a distance, in another monastery, must not have faced any of the issues faced by the monks, I could say it with certainty.

Since the trickle of women coming to meet me had become a flow, Mahanama got a pavilion built for us to sit together, like we did at Queen Pajapati's court. This open pavilion was near the orchards, at the far end of the palace grounds. It had rooms for me and Rohini to sleep in, if we wanted to, which we did most times. Narayani stayed in her own quarters in the palace but came over to the pavilion at sunrise.

The place was like an oasis in wilderness. Stray deer would come once in a while up to the windows of my room; peacocks were always strutting about royally, as though telling all and sundry that we were still in the royal grounds, which was true. Rabbits and squirrels abounded, entertaining the women who congregated at the pavilion.

Waking up with nature was not only a pleasure but therapeutic as well.

I cherished these early morning moments when nature seemed extremely busy yet imparted a peaceful calm, a sense of deep security, just like a mother.

The leaves would wake up and shake off their dewdrops; the insects would wake up and start flying or scurrying about to gather food; the birds would wake up and start waking up their family members by calling out to them, creating quite a cacophony; the buds would wake up and open up their petals; the flowers would wake up and raise their heads to welcome the sun.

Alone Again » 183

So many activities, yet so perfectly orchestrated. And the colours! So many of them, yet no two of them were the same shade—whether it was red or yellow or purple, each family of flowers had a different hue. And as far as the leaves were concerned, the shades of green were as countless as the stars in the sky.

It was amazing to see all this wondrous drama unfold, while just sitting in the garden.

One such morning, it struck me that when hundreds of thousands of creatures can live in harmony in nature, why can't us humans? I decided to talk to Anand about Devdutt and Kokalika. He had never talked about the latter, or mentioned that there was any strife amongst the monks.

I got my opportunity soon enough.

'Tell me about Kokalika today, Anand,' I said when he visited two days later. He was slightly thrown off.

'People like Kokalika are irrelevant, Your Grace. I like to talk to you about the Buddha's teachings, which are more relevant.'

'A few days ago, your brother Anirudh visited us. He mentioned some discord amongst the monks,' I insisted.

'Arguments and conflicts keep arising and then dissipating, like bubbles in water. In the past few years, the number of monks has increased manifold, and so have the monasteries. All of us have been given duties and responsibilities to carry out. The elders are always there to guide us, because the Buddha cannot be present everywhere.

'Sometimes some people do not agree with the Buddha's precepts and discuss it with him. But when his precepts are being taught by another elder, in another monastery, and some people disagree, then the Buddha is not there at that time to put their doubts to rest. Such doubts, when spread, become unsavoury. Anyway, all these things are a part of growth. When a tree is growing bigger and bigger, its purpose is to give fruit and shade to as many people as possible. During this time, some of its fruits or leaves might decay and fall off, but that does not hamper the ultimate purpose of the tree.'

Listening to Anand talk like this filled me with warmth. The quiet little boy had grown, and how!

'Actually, at the mention of disharmony, I remembered you mentioning some story about Kokalika, and that he and Devdutt were pretty close to each other. So, I surmised that given Devdutt's feelings towards Siddharth, maybe he is behind the friction within the sangha,' I pursued my line of enquiry.

'As far as Devdutt is concerned, he is one of the brightest and most capable of our seniors, as vouched by Master Sariputra too, in public. Unfortunately, this is the root of the problem,' Anand finally warmed up to the topic.

'Though we are not supposed to make our individual groups, since it goes against the very premise of a sangha, somehow a few monks have gravitated towards Devdutt, resulting in a mini sangha within the sangha. Kokalika, Khandadeviputra, Samudradutt and Katamoraka are part of that mini sangha. Out of them, Kokalika has now become the self-appointed attendant of Devdutt. This also happened because, being very talkative, Kokalika would be reprimanded by all the elders except Devdutt,' Anand concluded with a smile.

This was so typical in any royal court, I mused. There would always be rival factions, dissenters, a group of ministers who would disagree with the king. The court of Kapilvastu would have cramped Siddharth for sure. His court was the entire world, it was obvious now.

I could foresee Devdutt trying to displace or even oust Siddharth from his own sangha. There was no kingdom, no throne, nor king…yet…Devdutt was just being Devdutt. And soon enough, I was proved right. Though I could never have imagined even in my wildest of dreams that he would actually try to kill Siddharth, not once but thrice! I will come to this part of the story later.

One early morning, as I sat on the grass outside the pavilion, waiting for the dawn to break, an unusual visitor greeted me. It was Kisa.

'Welcome, Kisa. It has been many years since you came here. I hope all is well with you and Queen Pajapati. How is she keeping?'

Kisa had accompanied my mother-in-law and the other ladies in their quest for the Buddha, and now lived with her at their monastery in Vaishali. Once Queen Pajapati took her under her wing, Kisa vowed to look after her till her last breath. So, it was a bit odd to see her alone like this.

'Mahapajapati, as that's what we call her now, is gravely ill. We all are doing our best but feel that her life is ebbing away slowly. Lately, she has been talking about you a lot. She keeps wondering why it is not possible for you to commit fully to the Buddha's path and practices. What if the Buddha, when he visited last, had said, "Come, let us go out there and teach our shared path together"—would you have come then?'

'But he didn't, did he?'

I decided to accompany Kisa immediately. I wanted to attend to Pajapati and be with her through her death.

By the time we reached Pajapati's sanctuary, a small alms-house in the sprawling bamboo grove monastery, the sun had already set. From an overcast sky, the moon peeped every now and then. The hush of the night was broken only by odd sounds of crickets and other nocturnal insects.

Pajapati lay in her modest room, looking frail and exhausted, exaggerated further by the flickering amber candlelight highlighting her sunken eyes. The two nuns attending to my mother-in-law moved away when I reached her bedside. I sat by her head, stroked her forehead and cheeks and cradled her hand. It reminded me of the time when she did the same to me nearly two decades ago, when I was beside myself at being abandoned by the one and only love of my life.

Pajapati opened her eyes on my touch. Her eyes were as full of loving kindness as they were then. Holding hands, we remembered and talked about our lives together. She spoke about the sadness of a mother dying far away from her son. The Buddha and his monks were travelling in a different region, and had stayed there because of the rains.

Pajapati reminisced about the death of her sister Maya, and how she found refuge from that loss in looking after her sister's baby. The energies of her grief turned into a powerful protective force for the motherless baby, perhaps unconsciously wanting him to never ever face any grief of loss. How it backfired.

'Maya gave birth to Siddharth, not for her own sake, but for others, to drive away the suffering that comes with sickness and death. When I held the seven-day-old baby to my bosom, I knew that my life was meant to be surrendered to him.' Pajapati closed her eyes, her breathing rapid and shallow, shoulders straining, and sweat beading on her brow.

More nuns came in and we all tended to Mahapajapati, rubbing the soles of her feet and palms of her hands to give them warmth, gently wiping off the beads of perspiration from her forehead...a flow of deep love and gratitude was palpable. Inadvertently, a small circle of compassion was created around my mother-in-law.

Kisa relived her time meeting us at the palace. It was the death of her son that had led her to us, and to the Buddha: 'I understood the truth of impermanence. It is not just the truth of one village or town, or a single family; it is the truth of all living things, the core of all existence,' she said, folding her hands, bowing in gratitude.

'Your experience with your son and the mustard seed is not only about your insight into the impermanence of life; it is a lesson for us all. How did you get the insight? Your sharing of your pain and desperation with the villagers, and hearing their stories, opened your heart. When you stepped out from your isolation into the community, when you sat with us to share your grief, and to listen to ours, we were healed, as were you. It was compassion and insight co-arising among us. It did not happen alone, but with others.'

I was adamant in my belief that we all get our insights at different times, but being together with others helps us reach that goal faster. It was something that I had not only experienced myself, but also seen others like Kisa experience. Our sangha was born in releasing the *Me* by embracing the *We*.

Pajapati, oscillating between stupor and consciousness, opened her eyes and directed them at me. 'I believe deep in my heart that you have never yet been fully released from the suffering you went through on separation from your husband and your son. You are trying hard to keep alive your path of shared compassion, which is a tough path. My love and blessings are always with you. Channa told me that you are writing a journal. I am glad, as now I'm sure you will be heard.'

It was the first instance of my mother-in-law agreeing with what I was doing, even though I knew she did not agree fully with the path I was following. I did not mind that. As a mother, she was probably more comfortable and perhaps more confident following her son.

As though hearing my thoughts, Pajapati asked, 'Did I ever tell you a story about my past life?'

Of course she hadn't! We all gathered closer to her.

'I have been mother, son, father, brother and grandmother, too, in my past lives. Just like a river, I have flowed on from one life to another, till I could reach this one. In one of those lives, I saw a woman being ordained as a nun by the holiest of holy sages of that time. I aspired to be like her one day. Out of the many, two of my lives were crucial in bringing me to this present stage.' There was a renewed vigour in Pajapati's voice as she narrated her story.

'I was once a slave and lived on the outskirts of the city of Benares. We were five hundred of us women slaves, and I was the chief. One day, on the way back from the city, I came across five holy men. They looked tired, so I gave them water. On asking, they said that they were looking for some help in building their huts, but were disappointed. The rains were about to begin, and they had no place to stay. I took those sages to my village…' Pajapati paused to catch her breath.

'After eating and resting around the fire, I told the other slave women that we should help these holy men. They agreed, and we set out to get wood. In one night and day, we were able to build five huts for the five sages. For the next three months of rains, we looked after the holy men, gave them food and wove cloth for their robes. But something must still have been lacking. I was born again in a weaver's family in Benares. In that life, I fed five hundred sages who were returning hungry, having found no food in the city. Finally, I was born in this life as the foster-mother to the Buddha, and was ordained as the first nun by him. Carrying my desire to follow him from many lives, I had to but follow him in this one too.'

This resolved any unasked query that I had of Pajapati following her son's path.

My own suffering was my own hell, but it birthed a path for me, a different path from that of the Buddha. I was happy following it, and knew that it was important for me to clarify my stance to my mother-in-law before she passed on.

'You have joined the Buddha's sangha and embraced his teachings,' I addressed Pajapati as well as other familiar faces, 'but in the eleven years before you joined, our own path to awakening grew out of our shared suffering, our loss, our grief, and then our finding our way together. Meanwhile, the Buddha was on his own path of awakening, far away, alone.'

I could see that I had grabbed the attention of all the nuns.

'Now, after the few years that I have known about and observed the Buddha's path, outside of this sangha, the same as you have done within this sangha, we have all come to understand and benefit greatly from his teachings. But…' and here I could see some discomfort creeping in among my audience, 'but in my experience, my path and my practice, I sense something else, which is still unseen by the monks…' I paused for my words to sink in, as I was going to voice my deepest belief in public for the first time.

'…Siddharth, the Buddha, achieved freedom by leaving, by going forth alone, and then taking others along. Whereas my path, our path, was in staying, in learning to be with each other more and more deeply, and then going forth together. It taught us to live together, as a family, as a community.

'I am not renouncing any of the Buddha's teachings…' I added hurriedly. 'I am adding to them…showing that there is another way to enlightenment—a way of walking together, on a path, a shared path, that leads to the same place. Because I feel that every human deserves to have a chance to awaken, and not just the ones who are able to get away from their homes.'

There was a palpable silence following this, thick enough to be sliced like a fruit. Everyone seemed a little shaken, a little unsure…which to me meant that they believed in what I had said, and probably agreed too.

The silence was suddenly shattered by Pajapati's rasping cough that made everyone refocus their attention on her. Word had already been sent to the Buddha about his mother's deteriorating condition.

I sat at my mother-in-law's bedside for a week, watching her breath slow down gradually, her fluttering eyes open less and less frequently, till finally they closed for the last time. As Pajapati entered the realm of the deathless, I felt truly orphaned.

Queen Pajapati was cremated on a sandalwood pyre, just like her husband King Shuddhodhan, by their son Siddharth the Buddha. The sky thundered and the earth rumbled, as Pajapati was released by fire.

Watching from a distance, it struck me that we believe fire to be one of the five natural gods to whom we turn for purification. All religious ceremonies and rituals involve fire-worship. At the same time, somehow we also believe hell to be a pit of fire. If that were so, then hell's fire should have a cleansing or a purifying effect.

I remember my father telling me that all metals were purified by fire, as the heat destroyed or melted out the impurities.

In life, we equate hell with suffering, indescribable suffering, when our entire life seems to contract and become focused on the cause of our agony. This was exactly how I had described my life after Siddharth left.

'You have never yet been fully released from the suffering you went through on separation from your husband...' My mother-in-law's words seemed to echo in the crackling of the enflamed sandalwood, reminding me of the fire of my angry hell. It was yet another breakthrough moment for me. With folded hands, I bowed my head in gratitude to Pajapati, who in her own burning, showed me a mirror to save me.

I was fully released and relieved now.

The fire of my suffering had indeed purified me. My path was visible to me more clearly than ever now. When Siddharth left me, he closed the door to our shared quest into the meaning of life, our shared life. I had felt terrifyingly alone. Today, his mother Pajapati left, showing me that I had built another door for myself.

I was alone again, but at peace with myself.

12

LAST MEETING

I returned to Kapilvastu with thoughts of the various herbs I wanted to plant, once the rains stopped. Strangely, I was not thinking of my mother-in-law's passing at all. We had had a good conversation before she died, and I firmly believed that she had accomplished the purpose of her current birth.

It had become clear to me a while back that unless the images of our parents, children, relatives or friends are dissolved from our minds, we are unable to see our true selves. Once those images fade away and our minds turn inwards, we can reclaim our inherent strength that allows us to handle or deal with life's problems much more efficiently. Having done that, I now felt more in control and less thrown by unforeseen or unwanted events.

With Pajapati gone, my last bond with the material world was also gone. It was not that I was attached to her in the usual way of how familial relationships work; I had become detached from the material world long back. For me, it had more to do with the cultural make-up of the times. A subconscious part of us always felt responsible or duty-bound to the elders of our family. Pajapati was the last of the elders of my family.

At the risk of seeming rude, I must still mention that a kind of buoyancy had entered my being. I was looking forward to working with my plants again and started planning my routine.

A major thing I decided on returning was to shift completely into my rooms at the pavilion.

King Mahanama was worried about the heat of the summer bothering me, as the pavilion was not equipped with any cooling systems. The palace had an elaborate system of hidden waterways cooling the stone walls in summer. I suggested we use thatch to cool my rooms at the pavilion and planted flowering vines of different varieties of jasmine next to the walls, such that they could climb up to cover the walls all the way to the roof. The leafy cover provided the requisite coolness as well as protection from the direct heat of the sun's rays.

Rohini also moved in with me, and so did a few more maids, since Mahanama insisted on building more rooms behind the main pavilion. He also converted the winter palace into a monastery for nuns. The summer palace was already done up for the monks, as I had mentioned earlier.

As far as I was concerned, I was happiest living amidst nature. I had noticed that I was able to, by mere touch, heal the sick plants too...like an old magnolia tree that had stopped flowering, or a copse of bamboo that had stopped growing further. I would touch the sick plants tenderly and sit beside them, and I would talk to them as I would to any human. Sure enough, the plants or trees would be healed.

This confirmed my opinion that all living things have the same common life force running through them, and that they all benefit from tender loving care.

I had also developed a keen intuition about the healing properties of plants, even of those that my grandmother or mother had never told me about. I knew instinctively what grasses, flowers, seeds, leaves, fruits or even bark cured aches or fevers, alleviated digestive complaints, healed wounds or sores, or drove away sadness or nightmares and made one sleep like a child.

Word started spreading about my mysterious gift of healing and drew more people towards my pavilion. Not only women but men too started coming to me with their ailments. It turned into a deluge. Ultimately I had to put my foot down. I declared that I would visit the neighbouring villages and heal people in their homes. That gave me a chance to talk to the entire family and, more often than not, I would discover, and they would realize, the source from where their problems had sprung.

Rohini accompanied me, and we carried our bags of herbs and went visiting every morning. In the afternoon, we would return, eat and rest. Evenings would be spent talking with women in our circle of compassion. But that circle had grown and developed into an entity of its own. It did not necessarily need my presence. Sitting together in a circle, on fresh grass under a clear sky, somehow empowered the women, as though the shape of the circle itself generated energy. It was as though the Earth Goddess was blessing them.

I noticed another interesting development during our

morning visits. The ones suffering from terminal illnesses, who could not be cured, felt their pain and suffering ease when I sat with them and held their hands.

One afternoon, on our return, we found Kisa at the hermitage—that's what I had started calling the pavilion now, since more rooms had been added to it.

'How have you been, dear Kisa? It's been quite some time now since Mahapajapati left. Have you been to Vaishali since?'

'Things are not the same without Mahapajapati; they can never be. A number of nuns have joined, some of whom are queens. At the same time, the number of untouchables has also increased. Some women followers have not joined but became lay disciples, and look after us when we visit their towns, or help by getting shelters made for us. In fact, recently a sprawling mango grove has been gifted to us by Vaishali's famous courtesan Amrapali.'

'Oh, I have heard about Amrapali. Has she become a nun too?'

I didn't want to divulge what I had heard about her, as I believed it to be idle gossip. But it would certainly surprise me to learn that she had abandoned her luxurious lifestyle. She was considered the most beautiful woman in the country, and was pursued by all the rich men of Vaishali and nearby towns. It was said that men bearing riches in their carriages would be queuing outside her palatial mansion. I had even heard that King Bimbisar was very fond of her, and so was his son Ajatshatru, which naturally did not go down well with either of them.

Coming back to the cause of this drastic change in

Amrapali, I prodded Kisa to tell her story, and she obliged happily.

It happened just before the previous rainy season. A monk passing by Amrapali's mansion chanced to look up and seeing her standing in the balcony, stopped and bowed to her in respect. This was unusual for Amrapali as she was always surrounded by men who vied with each other to bid for her beautiful body. After all, being a courtesan, her job was to please men and satisfy their carnal needs.

Amrapali had only witnessed lust, and perhaps admiration for her beauty, in the eyes of all the men she had met, never respect. She ran out to meet him. 'Don't go away, be my guest today.'

'Your house seems to be full of rich and important people,' the monk gestured towards the carriages standing outside. 'My place is not with them. I am just a simple monk.'

'Please don't refuse my invitation, as it is the first time ever that I have invited someone to my house. I have been invited hundreds of times by kings, but I have never invited anyone. This is my first invitation, don't hurt me by refusing it. Come and have a meal with me'

The monk agreed and accompanied her into her house. Amrapali served the monk herself. Then she requested him to stay in her house in the forthcoming rainy season.

The monk said that he would have to talk to his master, the Buddha, about it. Only if the Buddha permitted could the monk stay at Amrapali's house.

When the monk met the Buddha and told him his story, to the surprise of everyone present there, he was given permission to stay at Amrapali's house for the three months of the rains.

Naturally, this resulted in a furore. All the monks unanimously felt that living with the courtesan would corrupt the monk, and his years of devotion to the Buddha's path would be wasted.

The Buddha simply said, 'We all will be here when he returns after three months. We will discuss this matter then. Let us just wait and watch; it would be a test of fire for him.'

To everyone's shock, the monk returned after three months with a woman dressed in yellow robes and introduced her as Amrapali, the famous courtesan of Vaishali, who wanted to be ordained as a nun. She offered her entire wealth, her mansion and a huge mango orchard to the Buddha, to be used by the monks and nuns.

'So now Amrapali lives like us, with us,' concluded Kisa with a flourish.

Amrapali falling in love with the monk reminded me of the time I fell in love with Siddharth.

The monk must have been carrying the light of compassion within him like a lamp carrying the flame, just like Siddharth. Like me, Amrapali also must have fallen in love with that luminance. If the monk had succumbed to Amrapali's charms, his light would have disappeared, and she would have found an ordinary man, like all other men around her, with no value. The value was in the monk's luminosity.

Such was the power of the monk's light that it lit a courtesan's heart. Amrapali surrendered herself at the feet of the Buddha, as he was the actual source of the monk's luminance.

Retrospectively, I felt that it was good that Siddharth had left when he did. I had no business containing his luminosity for myself alone. His light belonged to the entirety of mankind.

'It is good to know that the Buddha's words are spreading far and wide. It's also heartening to see people contributing to this endeavour of his by donating their wealth for the welfare of the monks and nuns. After all, they are the foot soldiers of the Buddha's army!'

'Oh yes, indeed!' Kisa agreed. 'There are others, kings, noblemen, merchants, and even some wealthy women, who have been instrumental in building rest houses, meditation halls and living quarters for monks and nuns to live during the three months of monsoon rains. Other than monasteries, smaller places for meditation have also been built by the rich followers of the Buddha. These places are for getting together, for discussing his path and precepts. In Rajgriha alone there must be a dozen such places,' she added.

The trickle had turned into a flow, and I could see it turning into a wave in the very near future.

'And there's an important bit of news that had almost slipped my mind,' Kisa flushed in excitement. 'The monks have started eating meat!'

I was aghast to hear this, to say the least, as Siddharth had always discouraged his cousins and friends from eating any sort of animal, bird or fish.

I was still trying to process this information in my head, when Kisa started explaining.

'The monks have to beg for their food, which they do only once a day. They have no control nor any choice over what they are being given. A monk has to accept everything gratefully, as the food he is given enables him to continue to live a monk's life. By accepting the alms, the monk is also enabling the giver to walk on the path of dharma. By refusing to accept, the monk would push the alms-giver from doing any form of charity in the future.'

An interesting way of looking at things, and why should it surprise me! This was Siddharth's typical way of analysing a situation. Very pragmatic.

The inference drawn was that if the monks were given meat as alms, they could not refuse. They had to eat it. The salient point was that since the animal was not killed at their behest, nor was it killed especially for them, it was not as if they had participated in killing a living being. So, they could still continue teaching non-violence while partaking in meat as alms.

Intriguingly, when the people who ate meat and offered it as alms heard the discourses of the Buddha about not taking life—from the very monks to whom they had given meat—they started reflecting on their own actions and attitude to meat-eating. In the larger picture, the monks accepting and eating meat seemed a small price to pay, since it actually resulted in creating more awareness, or maybe I should say guilt, in people about taking a life to satisfy their palate.

'I have been hearing so much about your work with women that I wanted to become a part of it,' Kisa said softly, sounding a tad hesitant.

'We would love to have you, Kisa! You were always a great help, not only to Mahapajapati but also to me. I remember how the women loved to listen to you, and how they went back healed and happy.'

I reminded Kisa of her time with me, before she left with my mother-in-law. More than me, Kisa would talk to the women; they related to her on a personal level, while with me they related only with my pain.

Rohini was visibly excited at the prospect of having Kisa stay with us. Most of her friends had gone in lots to join Pajapati, while she had decided to stay on with me. And I preferred silence to human company. Her sister Narayani also preferred to stay in the staff quarters of the palace. So, you see, Kisa being quite the babbler was bound to be a great companion to Rohini.

Leaving the two women to catch up and exchange notes, I moved on to check the bamboo enclosure where we were building birdhouses and small pond-like water bodies for birds.

Sparrows, magpies, koels, kites, parakeets and even owls had started visiting our little hermitage. By creating water bodies, I hoped to see some water fowls too. I had especially planted blueberry bushes in the bamboo enclosure, so our avian visitors would never go hungry.

I loved to watch the frolicking birds chattering away, splashing about water, or nibbling at berries with their stilted puppet-like bobbing heads. How free they were…I would muse…free to go anywhere, stop anywhere, eat anywhere, rest anywhere, be friends with everyone…

Whatever made humans feel so superior about their

being born as humans, I wondered. The animals seemed so much more at peace, as compared to us humans. The intelligence that we are so proud of had, thus far, only successfully created more and more shackles for us.

As a baby, Rahul was unaware that his father had left. In fact, he didn't even miss me as long as the wet nurse fed him. Even later, as a toddler, he was surrounded by a doting community of adults fulfilling his every need. In a sense, he was like any animal baby, free to move in the direction from where love flowed towards him. The birds were doing the same.

It was only when Rahul was grown up enough to make friends and play with them that the idea of a father or, for that matter, any relationship, entered his head. This is how we entangle ourselves, unknowingly, unconsciously absorbing the words spouted by people around us. And we do the same to others. Like a confused spider, we keep getting stuck in the web we weave ourselves.

Siddharth realized this the moment Rahul was born... the web was growing, growing tighter. He decided to break away. And it was good that he did. How else would I have found meaning in my life! Like many of my lives before, this life too would have gone to waste.

Four decades later, I still found myself thinking of Siddharth in any and every context. Marriage was indeed the thread that bound me with him forever, from many lives before to this life, and maybe more in the future... He was an invisible presence in my life, an impermanent permanence, or should I say a permanent impermanence!

The other day, someone had come from Rajgriha,

and they spoke about how frail in health the Buddha had become. I could imagine the regular cross-country travelling on foot taking its toll on Siddharth's physical health. Fortunately, Amrapali's son Jeevak was a physician and looked after the monks' health and well-being. He had also donated his mango grove to the sangha and lived close by Siddharth.

I was told that Jeevak had taught the basics to the monks regarding food and water, like not consuming leftover food from the previous day, and seeing to it that the water was clean before drinking it. He had also taught them to handle minor injuries, cuts and scrapes that the monks would invariably get while travelling through wooded terrain.

One morning, Anand came by with a young monk called Svasti, who must have been if not as old as Rahul, then maybe a couple of years older. I instantly remembered the buffalo incident involving Rahul and Svasti, narrated some time back by Anand.

'Looking at you, I'm reminded of my own son Rahul...'

'We are good friends. In fact, he is my only friend in the sangha. He has told me a lot about you and his life before he joined the sangha. That was why I requested Master Anand to take me with him, when I learnt he was going to visit you,' young Svasti beamed from ear to ear.

'A lot about his life! Rahul had barely touched seven when he left us to be with his father. Not much of a life he had to talk about,' I laughed.

Svasti seemed a bit embarrassed at my comment, but seeing Anand and me laughing heartily, he relaxed.

'The Buddha is doing fine, though he lacks the strength

he had a decade ago. He has to rest his back against a wall now while giving his discourse, but mentally he's as sharp, if not sharper than before.'

'Thank you, Anand, for letting me know. Though Siddharth is as old as me, his body has gone through much more physical hardship in the last forty years than mine. Maybe he should think about stationing himself at a place rather than travelling so much. Or, if he has to travel, then maybe a palanquin would be a better option than walking. He should perhaps think about getting someone else to deliver discourses...'

'Devdutt suggested that the Buddha should take it easy now and hand over the responsibility of the sangha to him,' Anand paused, as though to gauge my reaction to this.

I had no comments to make. It had to be Siddharth's decision.

Of course, I knew that Devdutt, or for that matter anyone else, would not be able to replace the Buddha. No, I was not being partial. Siddharth had sacrificed everything to find the way out of suffering; he spoke and taught from his personal experience and understanding. Anybody else would at best be a weak copy of him. Siddharth's sheer honesty, his conviction in his own doctrines, and his compassion and receptiveness towards every living being, attracted people to him. They listened to him and their lives changed for the better. Who could match that charisma?

'The Buddha said that heading the sangha was a huge responsibility that no one in his eyes was as yet capable of shouldering. In any case, the seniors were looking after the novices, and all of us had our own responsibilities to handle. Devdutt did not like this and left the sangha with his own band of followers, and moved to Gaya.'

'Are you saying that Devdutt has left for good?' It did not sound right. Devdutt was family.

'Yes, it pains me to say that my brother Devdutt has not only left the Buddha, but is also being fully supported by Prince Ajatshatru of Magadh, who himself wants to usurp his father's throne.

'Jeevak told us that King Bimbisar was imprisoned in the palace, and the entire plotting and planning was done by Ajatshatru with Devdutt's advice. Not only this, Devdutt also tried to get the Buddha killed three times. Once he sent a soldier to behead the Buddha while meditating. When that failed, he sent another one to roll a boulder down the mountain to kill the Buddha, but only his foot got hurt. Finally, a mad elephant was let loose on the Buddha while he was walking. Miraculously, the moment the elephant reached him, he became as docile as a lamb.'

Anand was always fond of narrating incidents, adding a dash of his magic to them. Nevertheless, Devdutt behaving in this way was beyond my comprehension. It sounded almost inhuman. So many years with the Buddha had done nothing to change his core.

I sincerely wished that Devdutt would introspect and find his hidden emotions and motives. They must be hidden still, because had he faced them, he would have understood them and dealt with them differently. Maybe he would have reasoned, or tried to reason, with Siddharth as to why he felt he should head the sangha. Trying to kill his own brother went against all possible precepts that Siddharth taught in his sangha. And Devdutt wanted to head the Buddha's sangha! It was sad that he could not see his own contradictory thoughts.

'I feel sad for Devdutt. He still hasn't grown up. Six decades hence, nearly a lifetime for some, and Devdutt remains the same child as what I remember from before my marriage.'

'Why child? If so, then isn't being like a child a good thing? One keeps hearing about childlike innocence in the Awakened Masters,' said Svasti, looking genuinely confused.

'That's a very sensible question, Svasti. You have heard right, the Awakened One has no judgement of what is good and what is bad, just like a child. How so, you might ask? A child can't distinguish between right–wrong, good–bad, as he has no experience. If your mind is clean like a child's, then naturally all judgement disappears. Hence, we say that every awakened person becomes a child again—innocent, yes, but certainly not ignorant.

'If life is lived rightly, with alertness, with joy, with silence, and with understanding, you not only grow old, you also grow up. Everybody grows old, but not everybody grows up. Devdutt has grown old but he hasn't grown up.'

Before leaving, Svasti turned, I think on an impulse, and asked if he could visit me again.

'Of course. You are welcome any time, son,' I said with a smile, and couldn't resist adding, 'with or without Anand.'

My writing continued as days merged into weeks and months and years. I stopped going out to visit families. I rarely sat with Kisa in their circle of compassion. All around me, I saw women, rarely men, coming and going, looking happy and at peace.

Kisa and Rohini were now joined by Anupriya, a young girl who had bravely walked away from an abusive marriage. Anu, as she was mostly called, was very good with young women. She taught them to become self-reliant, and she encouraged them to study. Anu also managed to single-handedly convince older women to not get their daughters married forcibly. I was grateful to her for showing the path to so many women. It was as though Pajapati's spirit had descended on this triad of Kisa, Rohini and Anu.

If King Shuddhodhan was pleased watching his son's rule from above, then Queen Pajapati mustn't be any less happy seeing how her work with women had grown and flourished.

I spent more and more time walking or sitting in nature, talking and listening to it. One morning, I discovered a peepal tree near the northern boundary of the palace grounds, just before the deep woods began. Strangely, I had never noticed it before. Maybe it was a sign of sorts. I recalled Siddharth telling me about his awakening under a peepal tree, on the banks of Niranjana River.

I decided to spend some time sitting under the peepal and listening to what it had to say to me.

As I sat under its comforting shade, I recalled my grandmother telling me that Saraswati, the goddess of wisdom, arose from a giant peepal tree, somewhere in the high unreachable Himalayan mountains. But I was more interested in hearing stories about powerful goddesses, like Kali. My child-brain could not correlate wisdom with power at that age. Now I wished I had listened to Saraswati's story.

Anyway, there were other coincidences that I could clearly see.

Siddharth's birth-mother Maya had seen an elephant as white as Himalayan snow upon the conception of her son. Maybe it did come from the Himalayas. Maybe the peepal tree is the vehicle for wisdom from the king of the mountains. Siddharth attained Buddhahood under a peepal. This peepal tree was growing in the northern periphery of the royal grounds, beyond which lay the dense woods, beyond which rose the mighty Himalayan ranges. Wasn't that a whole lot of signs trying to tell me something?

As I continued to look up at its twinkling foliage, I could see the bright sky peeping through. I could also see wispy cotton-like white clouds dotting the blue sky. As I enjoyed the gentle warmth of the filtered sunshine, I thought that in a few weeks' time these clouds would grow into darker, heavier versions of themselves, and bring rain to us, to this peepal tree. And like this, so many years must have gone by; so many times the sun must have shone and the clouds must have rained.

What about the wind? For years, the wind must have blown to carry the seeds of the peepal to and from places afar. Even this peepal tree must have grown from some seed carried by the wind from who knows where…when we sit under a tree, we enjoy its shade, maybe its fruits if they are edible, but do we ever think how all of it came about, with whose help? So much goes into the creation of everything. I had had a similar thought earlier too, about inter-dependence, once when I was sitting by the lotus pond.

This gigantic shady tree that grew out of a tiny seed, with the help of sunshine and rain, in the soil, was once a part of another peepal tree's fruit, and was carried here by the wind. So, was the tree born here? No, it was already existing in the seed that came here. That seed was a part of the tree which also came from a seed from elsewhere, and so on and so forth. So, was the tree born at all? It seemed to me that the peepal tree, or for that matter any tree, always existed somewhere else, in some other form. This was a never-ending saga.

It suddenly dawned on me that the peepal tree was not born, it was manifested. And hence, it couldn't die.

I lay down on the grass beneath the tree and continued looking above at the shimmering canopy of dancing leaves. Even without any perceptible wind, the leaves bobbed on their slender stems, their delicate, gently curved tips seemingly acting as rudders. I was mesmerized by the workings of nature.

Everything is in continuum. Nothing is born, so nothing can die. The clouds and rain are different manifestations of the same water—the clouds don't die, neither does the rain, they just keep changing their forms. Impermanence is the basic nature of everything.

Even our own identities, or those that we impart to others, are impermanent. The identity of a seed changes when it turns into a tree, and so on. And the source of all suffering is the false belief in permanence and the existence of separate selves.

All the distinctions of pure–impure, small–large, birth–death, and so many others are a creation of our mind, our intellect. Because of their false belief in permanence, people form attachments. And I knew from my personal experience how painful attachments could be.

Getting rid of my false beliefs had led me to freedom from suffering. Here, I don't mean freedom from physical pain, for pain is the nature of the body. It's the mental suffering that I was rid of. Letting Rahul go was not as painful as letting Siddharth go. Acceptance was the key, as well as giving up trying to avoid the inevitable. With self-acceptance, my inner strength had grown tremendously, and I could handle any difficult or trying situation without becoming distressed.

I lay there under the peepal, feeling as comfortable as on my bed, till the light started to fade. The evening star became visible. With that, another thought flashed in my mind. The stars stay wherever they are, the darkness stays too. When the sun lights up the sky, the stars, the darkness cannot be seen…but they are still there, they do not go anywhere.

Nothing is born, nothing dies. Everything just is.

I picked up a peepal leaf from the ground and walked back to my hermitage, firmly convinced of the fact that Siddharth must have had the same experience under the peepal tree as I did a while back. We always reached the same conclusions, however varied our paths might be.

It was like Siddharth and I were walking in the same direction but with a transparent wall between us. We were aware of each other's progress, though without actually meeting. We started at the same point, he went one way, I went the other, but eventually our journeys culminated at the same destination.

I felt that Siddharth followed his head, while I followed my heart. He would observe, think, analyse and reach a conclusion. He would even try and test the paths before he chose one. Meanwhile, I observed, yes, but instead of testing and analysing, I sensed the path within my heart intuitively. For me, it was like healing people—I was guided by my intuition more than my knowledge.

I was at peace, with myself and the world around me. There was nothing more left for me to discover or understand. I felt I was ready to leave for the next plane and decided to visit Siddharth and inform him. We had entered this world together. I owed it to him to inform him of my decision to leave it.

I looked around and saw many Kisas and Anus in the hermitage. In the royal precinct, between the two monasteries of the Buddha, our little place stood out like an oasis.

I was happy in the awareness that while the conditions were not ripe as yet for the full flowering of the shared path, I had still planted the seeds. They were bound to sprout one day…like the peepal.

There will definitely come a time; meanwhile, my job is done.

Farewell.

ACKNOWLEDGEMENTS

Acknowledging the journey this story has taken—from its embryonic stage to its fully realized form—I find myself indebted to numerous individuals who, often unwittingly, provided the fertile ground for its seed to germinate and grow.

Mrs Dham, my school librarian, stands out as one of those guiding lights. She allowed me to borrow a dozen books on a single card, indulging my fascination with encyclopaedias and reference books. My paternal grandfather deserves special mention for introducing me to a world of spiritual masters and philosophers, including the Buddha, through his remarkable personal library.

I am deeply grateful to my photographer friend Chiru, whose assistance enabled me to meet His Holiness the 14th Dalai Lama. My friends Arvind and Amitabh made our adventurous—and at times perilous—Buddhist pilgrimage an unforgettable experience.

Avdhesh, my husband, deserves special mention for not only holding the fort in my absence but also understanding my mood swings and my tendency to drop everything abruptly to pen down random thoughts while working on this story. My mother and my daughters, Shruti and Smriti, form my unwavering moral support system—the audience who I know will always cheer on my literary endeavours. In fact, my elder daughter, Shruti, dreams of seeing this story on the big screen—Hollywood no less!

Here, I must share a cherished memory involving my younger daughter, Smriti. As she was leaving for New York to pursue her graduation, we were all teary-eyed, watching the youngest member of our family, still a teen, prepare to venture far away on her own. In the midst of this emotional moment, she said, 'Mom, now that I'm through with school, you must get back to your Buddha story.' The fact that this thought occurred to her at such a time speaks volumes. It remains one of my favourite go-to memories, a poignant reminder of her faith in me and this journey.

Special thanks to my friends Rajeev and Abhishek of Motilal Banarsidass Publishing House, for granting me full access to their phenomenal collection of Buddhist studies, many of which now grace my own library. I am equally grateful to Dr Charles Willemen, professor at the International Buddhist College, Thailand, for introducing me to rare Buddhist texts unavailable in India, and for encouraging me to read between the lines and uncover the unseen.

I owe a debt of gratitude to Kapish Mehra, managing director of Rupa Publications, and Rudra Sharma, my commissioning editor, for their unwavering encouragement to tackle challenging subjects that pushed me out of my comfort zone.

Lastly, I am forever grateful to my readers and the publishers who have supported me over the years. Your continuous acceptance and appreciation have been the cornerstone of my journey as an author. Thank you for making this dream possible.